QUANTUM ENTANGLEMENT

PART ONE

LEGION OF SUPERNATURAL ACADEMY

USA TODAY BESTSELLING AUTHORS
S.R. WATSON & RYAN STACKS

Quantum Entanglement: Part One (Legion of Supernatural Academy Series)

Copyright © 2019 S.R. Watson & Ryan Stacks

www.watsonandstacks.com

Cover Design: Joolz & Jarling Book Covers

Editor: Editing4Indies

Photo Credit: RplusMphoto

Cover Model: Ryan Stacks

PROLOGUE

Series Foreshadow

What is the meaning of life? That is the big question, and it truly is a complex debate. It's a question for a higher power, no doubt. The world has multiple opinions, but one idea makes the most sense. The idea parallels human emotion and the workings of the universe. This idea is that we were created for relationship, created for love. It's hard to ignore all the signs the universe puts right in front of us. Love can be seen on a large scale as well as a subatomic scale. It can cross worlds and feel almost magical. It can be found across time and throughout every living species. Everywhere you look, love is a natural thing. It's in you, and it's in me; it's in our chemistry. But we all view love as something different based on our experience with it. These experiences could be blissful, painful, or even unknown. But it's a feeling that helps a species survive. All humans are 99% the same even though we have come to believe we are all so different from one another. Yet some out there are different than others. They are special. Something along the lines of "supernatural." Special or not, we all have so many moments that happen in our life appear to us as unpredictable. But what if these stories weren't as unpredictable as they seemed? What if the world was exactly just that...? A story. Our lives could already be pre-planned. Every action has already been written on paper. What if every person we are supposed to come in contact with was held together within the pages of this book? Every life we are destined to touch has already been determined. One will begin to wonder if their life is really their own. These are the mysteries we all live with on the daily. Some will question the secrets of the world, but few will get the opportunity to discover the truth.

CHAPTER ONE

Genesis

"Are you on drugs?"

Wait ... what? The question is so asinine, it borders on insulting. I'm probably the most strait-laced person he knows at this university.

"Genesis, are you even listening to me?" Cooper tries again to get my attention. He's been my boyfriend since last semester, but the past few days of our relationship have been shaky at best.

"Yes, I'm listening, and no, I'm not on drugs. What kind of question is that, anyway?"

"The kind that tells me you haven't been listening to a word I've said." His voice escalates a bit, causing me to look around the crowded campus coffee shop. "You've been avoiding going out with me, and when I do manage to get you out of your dorm, I get this version of you —distant."

I tug at the Ace bandage on my left wrist, knowing

he's right. We've been growing apart for a while, and I'm just tired of pretending. "Well, I've been buckling down for exams. The semester just started, and I don't want to piss away the GPA I've worked all these years to earn. We're seniors now. There's no room for error if I want to graduate with honors next semester," I argue.

He rolls his eyes at my futile attempt at an excuse. "That's not it. You study more than anybody I know and have aced every exam up to this point. Don't bullshit me. If you've grown tired of our relationship, then just tell me."

I tug at the bandage once more as my teeth gnaw at my bottom lip. I don't know what else he wants me to say —that I'm spiraling? That unexplainable stuff is happening to me, and I think I'm losing my mind? Unexpectedly, he stills my arm on the table while simultaneously unwrapping the bandage. Before my brain can acknowledge that he's about to reveal one of my reasons for concern, the bandage lies in a heap in front of him. I grab my wrist, but he pries my hand away. *Too late.*

"What the hell is this?" he asks, now staring down at the infinity symbol embedded into my flesh and raised like a brand.

The truth is, I have no answers. It wasn't there three nights ago. I woke up in a cold sweat—disoriented and naked at Lake Chelan. I had no recollection of how I got there or how I did so without clothes. Worst yet, I had lost a whole day. The last thing I remembered was attending class here at the University of Washington, and then I woke up almost two hundred miles away. I don't do drugs, but had someone roofied me? I've been a basket case ever since, trying to make sense of it all. How do I explain that to someone? How do I decipher between the ugly choices that either I'm losing my mind, or I was intentionally abducted for ill purposes? Steve and Jan had to come pick me up. They're my adoptive parents ... a fact that was kept from me until it was time for me to go off to college. Replacing their titles of mom and dad with their first names is my rebellion. My whole life has been a lie. Still, they were the ones I called to come and get me. Fear overrode logic and grudges. I needed them. What if my birth parents were mentally unstable? Was this a sign of a manifestation within me? I dare not tell the guy I've been dating for the past six months that I may be certifiably batshit crazy.

"Dammit, Genesis. You're doing it again, and I'm beginning to think it's intentional."

The sharp edge in his tone has me pulling my arm away from him. "I don't know. I don't remember," I confess honestly.

"I can't believe you're lying to me. Either you're doing drugs and don't remember getting your wrist branded, or you just don't want to tell me. Either way, you're not the woman I thought you were."

"What are you saying?" I ask nervously. The words nearly get caught in my throat.

"I'm saying I've had enough of your flaky behavior and

lies. Tell me what you're hiding from me, or this is over." He gestures back and forth between the two of us.

"I went to my parents' house in Spokane this past weekend."

"And ...?"

"And that's all I remember." I leave out the part about waking up naked at a lake.

"What do you mean, that's all you remember? How did you get this?" he asks, grabbing my arm and turning it over once again.

"I don't know, and that's the truth. Take it or leave it."

"I couldn't have said it better myself. I'll leave it. Thanks for wasting six months of my time."

By this time, the stares around the small coffee shop are unmistakable. Some of the students have the decency to pretend they aren't fully engaged in our shitshow but others, not so much.

"Whatever ... good riddance," I dismiss with false conviction. I slam my fists on the table before us, and the room goes still.

I mean *literally. Fucking. Still.* I slow blink a few times, willing myself to wake up. This has to be a dream—like the naked at the lake thing. The people in the coffee shop are frozen in whatever posture they were in before this phenomenon occurred. I slide my chair back from the table to stand, but nobody else moves. The clock's secondhand doesn't budge. The milk being poured into the latte behind the counter looks like it's in a solid state —midair. My eyes finally look toward the door where students pass casually along the sidewalk, oblivious to the mind fuck going on inside. What if someone comes in and witnesses this? What have I done? Why am I the only one who can move? Is any of this real? Thinking quickly, I pull out my phone to record it. I need proof that I'm not crazy and that this is actually happening. I record for a solid ten seconds, ready to run if anyone walks in. After I slide my phone back into the pocket of my jeans, I weave through the still frozen people toward the exit. I exhale once I'm finally outside. The splattering sounds of shit falling to the floor inside piques my interest. I look through the window at the now unfrozen students, shaking their heads in mutual confusion. Cooper looks around the coffee shop just as confused. I don't know what just happened, but I'm more than a little afraid of what these unsolved, unexplained events are escalating to. Even scarier is that I don't know how I go about finding out.

A man bumps into me on the sidewalk as I attempt to run away. "You need to come with me," he urges. Quickly perusing him, I find him blond, clean cut, and professionally dressed. Was he a professor here? Did he witness what just happened? He opens the door to the coffee shop. Leaning inside midway, he snaps his fingers at seemingly nothing before closing the door and looking me in the eyes. "I have the answers you seek ... Now come."

He begins to walk off, but I'm hesitant to follow. Who is this man, and what kind of answers does he have? It would be ludicrous to follow a stranger just because he said so. But then again, none of this is logical. I watch as his retreating back gets farther away from me as my own feet refuse to move. I'm the one frozen now. I'm conflicted. I want answers, but at what cost? I begin to take indecisive steps in the same direction as the stranger. *Left foot ... right foot*, one in front of the other, but my feet feel like lead. What am I doing? Am I really going to follow this man?

"Yes," a man's gruff voice answers inside my head. I shake it to clear it. "Don't be afraid. I know you can hear me, so please do as I say. And whatever you do, don't look back. Just keep following me."

Now I'm even more convinced I'm losing it. I want to look back, but I'm afraid. Being told *not to be afraid* is futile. This is not real life. "Where are you leading me? And why can't I look back?" I ask within my mind, desperate to see if the stranger can hear my thoughts once again.

"I promise to explain the logistics of it all, but for now, I need you to focus on what I'm going to tell you next. You're being followed. It's important they don't get a good look at your face."

I pause mid step. I need to see who is behind me. You can't tell someone not to look and expect them not to want to. Fear, however, is a hell of a deterrent. Compliance with his instructions doesn't dissuade me from conjuring all the horrible ways this can end, though. Is my life in danger? This man just read and answered my inner thoughts from at least thirty yards away. This doesn't comfort me. It petrifies me.

"Don't stop and don't look back," he warns again a little more sternly. He disappears to his left up ahead. "When you get to the Hillshire Bank, there is an alley to your left. Be ready to sprint toward the light. Your life depends on it."

He just confirmed the outcome my thoughts had wavered to. What word comes after petrified because that would be the rabbit hole that my feelings have sunk in to. *Run toward the light? My life depends on it?* Doubt and angst consume me. Still, I know I will follow his instructions to the letter. Whatever all these twilight happenings have been leading up to is currently unfolding. I can hear footsteps a little too close behind me now that I'm focused and hyper alert. My pace is brisk, so I'm definitely being pursued. Adrenaline pumps through my veins as my fight or flight response kicks in. I quicken my steps; the bank is in sight. The second I reach it, I sprint left toward the alley as the stranger instructed. A huge blinding light orb confines the narrow space. I no longer have time to think or second-guess whether I'm making a mistake. Running through it, I feel the instant the strange man grabs me by the shoulders to pull me through even more, but I'm distracted by the jolt of pain that pierces my body. It's unlike anything I've ever felt. *Excruciating.* He catches me as I fall limp into his arms. I'm at his mercy. My eyes slide closed as the light still dance behind my eyelids.

CHAPTER TWO

Elysian

The music thumps underneath my feet, echoing off the confined space of the gym. The university does offer a more state-of-the-art gym on the other side of the campus, but it's usually saturated with pretentious jocks more interested in showing off for the women than actually working out. My wrestling buddies and I prefer the privacy of this best kept secret. I continue to load more barbells onto the bar, but none of it seems sufficient. I bench press a few reps, growing frustrated by the minute. Not with the workout really, but with all the crap plaguing my thoughts—finals and the recent fire at my apartment. I went to bed after a night of partying and woke up to alarms blaring and my place going up in flames. Thankfully, my downstairs neighbor called 911 in time. Fire trucks were dispatched before the blaze could move on to the other units. The origin and cause for the fire have yet to be given, but

I'm freaked out about the dream I had prior to the incident. The specific details are hazy due the alcohol I consumed that night, but I remember shooting balls of fire from my hands. The why, at who, and how are the foggy bits. But how coincidental that I wake up to fire surrounding me and smoke so thick, the contents in my bedroom were no longer visible. The fireman didn't know how I escaped, and if I'm being honest, I don't know either.

"What the hell are you doing, bro?" My buddy Josh's voice interrupts my thoughts as I add another barbell onto the bar. "Going for some sort of record the team doesn't know about? That's some Olympic weight you got going on there. No way you're lifting that. Are you trying to injure yourself before wrestling season even starts?"

I look ... I mean really look at the bar for the first time since I started bench pressing. The amount of weight I have loaded makes my eyes bulge. I pushed out four reps before I decided it still wasn't enough weight on that last set. That means I just bench pressed 225 kg ... Shit, I just benched 495 lbs. I back away in awe. To say that is a personal best is an understatement. That would be the personal best of our entire Penn State wrestling team. I'm not an Olympic athlete, and I've never benched more than 275 lbs.

"I was just kidding around. I was going to snap a pic for inspiration. It's a goal I'm working toward."

I surprise even myself at how easily that lie rolls out of my mouth. The truth is, I have no logical explanation of how I was able to bench that much, so I'm going to pretend that I didn't. *For now.*

"Dude. That amount of weight is not necessary to get the job done. What *is necessary* is to keep you injury free so we can have another undefeated season." He shakes his head, and I can only grin at him as I pat him on the shoulder. He is one of my closest friends and not just because he's letting me crash on his sofa until I find another place.

"Crap, I gotta get going. If I'm late to Mr. Seymour's economic class one more time, he's going to kick me out. I need to take all the notes I can from this lecture because his last exam was almost word for word from my notes. Buying the textbook was a waste of money." I grab my backpack off the floor and throw it over my shoulder.

"You'll never make it." Josh chuckles behind me.

He isn't kidding. The economics building is across campus, and I only have a couple of minutes to get there. I take off in a sprint anyway. Maybe if I can minimize how much I'm late, I can arrive before he locks the door. I kick up dirt, grass, and debris as the wind whips through my drenched shorts and tank. I can only imagine what I must smell like as I plop into my seat, barely out of breath.

The students turn in their seat to stare at the disturbance because my entrance was anything but graceful. Beads of sweat drip down my chest and forehead. I wipe it away before realizing I still have my wrist straps on. I undo them, only to be met with another phenomenon—

an infinity symbol branded on my left wrist. When did that get there? It couldn't have been there before this morning ... could it? Before today's events and the fire, I would have allocated this to a college hazing gone wrong, but some freaky shit has been going on. Mr. Seymour interrupts my thoughts with the close of the door. It's one o' clock on the dot. I'm not late? How is that possible? I left the gym a couple of minutes to the hour. Is his clock wrong? I look down at my watch, and it reads the same time as the clock. How did I make it with time to spare? Too many unexplained things are happening with me—increased strength, speed, the brand, the fire. What's going on?

A white-haired man enters, and I can hear Mr. Seymour say, "I thought I locked that door."

The man's stoic expression never changes. His white hair is at odds with his youthful appearance, but so is his suit. What is the occasion? He looks directly at me as if reading my thoughts before quietly telling our professor the reason for his intrusion.

"Mr. Remis, it seems you're needed for an urgent matter. This gentleman is here to escort you and fill you in." Mr. Seymour gives the white-haired man a look over, unsure.

I waste no time grabbing my backpack off the floor. I stash my wrist straps in one of the front pockets before flinging it over my shoulder once more. Was it my mom and dad? Another family member? I wait until I'm outside the classroom before I turn to the stranger. "What is the urgent matter? Is my family okay?"

"Your family is fine. And yes, I was reading your thoughts back in there."

"What are you talking about?" I ask, now breathing a sigh of relief that he wasn't here about anything related to my family.

"Well, you were thinking that I was looking at you as if I was reading your thoughts. I was reading them."

"Look, I don't know what kind of game you're playing, but you have a few seconds to tell me the reason you pulled me out of my class, or I'm leaving you out here. What was so urgent?" I don't know what I was expecting him to say, but my relief is short-lived.

"The fire, the infinity symbol on your inner left wrist, and your increased speed and strength are all the reasons I'm here," he explains with a flat affect. Has this man been watching me? Oh, wait ... he read my thoughts, but how?

"No, I haven't been watching you. I was able to sense use of supernatural ability, which led me here to investigate," he answers the question in my mind. How the fuck did he do that? Supernatural what? "Look, we'll be here all day with your internal monologue of questions. A beacon has been sent, so it won't be long before others will come to investigate too. I can explain all of this to you, but we need to get you to a safe place first."

"Safe? Am I not safe now? Who am I in danger from?"

"Too many questions. Do you understand we need to

go now?" Two men appear at the end of the hall ... too far for me to get a good look at them, but if the urgency in Mr. White Hair's voice is any indication, this is the danger he was referring to. "Like right now. Cross your arms over your chest and hold on."

I do exactly as he says, too stunned to do anything else. The minute he grabs my shoulders, an orb of white light encircles us. My eyes are forced shut from the brightness, followed by stabbing pain. What the hell just happened? The pain pulses through me relentlessly until I succumb to total darkness.

CHAPTER THREE

Genesis

Light slowly begins to filter in as I blink and rub my eyes. "Ah." I gasp as a sharp pain makes me protest the sudden movement.

"Try not to move too much," the strange man suggests. "You just experienced your first joint teleportation. Your body went through quite an ordeal."

"A joint what? You're not making any sense, and the cryptic act is getting old. I followed you, endured whatever the hell that was, and now I want answers," I huff as I lie back on the hard surface.

"You just teleported with me. Teleportation is ..."

"I know what teleportation is, and there's no such thing. Did you roofie me? Drug me? Is this some kind of bad trip?"

"I can assure you I did no such thing. Look around ... what do you see?"

I look around, suspiciously—careful not to take my

17

eyes off him for too long. "We're in some kind of clinic. Why am I on an operating table?" I shriek when I realize what hard surface I'm lying on. I've seen enough of these on television.

"Calm down, I'm not going to hurt you. I could have already done so if that was my intent." He begins to pace, worry creeping into his handsome face for the first time. "It's just as I thought. You're a supernatural."

"Super what? Hello? Can you stop pacing, and tell me what you're going on about?" I sit up again too quickly, and the jolt of pain reminds me to settle the hell down.

"The thing you did in the coffee shop was a form of magic, Genesis." I want to ask him how he knows my name, but my brain is stuck on the *magic* part. He has my full attention. "Unsanctioned magic. It's against the rules to use magic or any supernatural ability in the presence of humans."

"Wait. I'm human. What are you talking about? And anything I did wasn't intentional. I don't know magic. I mean I know what supernatural is, but that's fiction ..."

"Genesis." He snaps his fingers, getting my attention. "Just listen. It's a lot to take in but try to listen so you can come to terms with it. Then I'll answer any questions you may have." My silence is his cue to continue. "I know your magic wasn't intentional, but it still sent off a beacon to other supernaturals. The two men who appeared when I said don't look back had come to investigate. Those men were shapeshifters. Werewolves," he clarifies.

"Am I ...?"

"No, you're not a werewolf," he answers. "They have a distinct smell, and you don't."

"I don't wholeheartedly buy into all this make-believe stuff, but I don't have logical answers either. So what am I?"

"That's what I brought you here to find out."

"And how are you going to find out? What are you going to do to me?" I ask nervously, looking around at all the medical equipment in the glass cabinets and on the countertops.

"Relax. I promised I wasn't going to hurt you. This is an old veterinary clinic out in the middle of nowhere. I cast a minor illusion spell to make it look like a secluded day spa to humans. The minute you correctly saw this place for what it actually is, I knew you were supernatural. That was the first test. Now we just need to determine what kind of supernatural being you are."

"Are you telling me that I'm not human? That you're not human? You said you casted a spell."

"No. My guess is that you're at least half human. Your pain receptors and regeneration are that of a human. It also explains why the joint teleportation was so painful for you. Teleporting two people requires more of an energy force. But the things I've listed so far rule out vampire since you have the ability to be out in sunlight."

He walks closer to the table to study me. Probably trying to gauge how far I am from flipping the hell out. If I wasn't in so much pain, I'm quite sure I would've hopped off this table already.

"Vampires? Werewolves? What else exists?" I can't wrap my head around any of this.

"All the things that go bump in the night. All the fairy tales and myths you were probably ever told." My eyes widen in complete fear. "Not all supernatural beings reside here on Earth, though. Only witches, warlocks, vampires, and shapeshifters."

"That's plenty, don't you think?" He lets out a hearty laugh, but I can't find the humor in it. I'm more afraid now than I was before he brought me here. *Teleported* me here. *Whatever.*

"Much like the democracy that's in place for humans, the supernaturals have their own governing body that establish rules to promote order. Then we have the outliers who insist on being the judge and jury independent of those rules. I'm Mr. Blakely, the headmaster of the Legion of Supernatural Academy." He smiles at me for the first time, but it's only somewhat reassuring.

"What do they do at this academy?" I prod.

"Well, after we have identified a supernatural being, we group them based on that classification. They learn to harness and develop their powers, the history of their ancestry, and most importantly, the rules so that they avoid being punished or banished for unsanctioned practices."

"Why did you bring me here then? Where is the academy? How long do I have to stay for?"

"Slow down. I brought you here first to identify what kind of supernatural being you are. I have to protect the students of the academy from the unknown."

"And I'm the unknown," I state as I slowly swing my legs around the table to slide off.

"Yes, for now. But we will run some tests, and once I'm comfortable that you're stable, and it's safe, I'll take you to the school."

"Well, give me your business card, and we can schedule some time to meet up to figure out what kind of *supernatural* being that I am," I say with air quotes. I still think this is all a bad dream. I need to see Steve and Jan.

"I don't think you understand. You can't go back out there like this. Your ability is unpredictable and out of control. If I had to guess, I'd say you've experienced some unexplainable events before you froze all those people in that coffee shop. If you're not careful, you can really hurt someone. I erased their memory of the event with a snap, but this is not going away. And yes, I broke a rule to rescue and get you here."

"Dammit. Don't say that. I have exams coming up. Thank you for breaking a rule for me, but I can't stay here." I lie back on the table and close my eyes so he can't see the tears welling in my eyes, but that doesn't stop them from spilling over. I feel his gentle thumb wipe them away.

"I know this is overwhelming, but I also know you don't want to risk hurting anyone. I can't protect you out there. Just work with me and we'll figure something out with your university so you don't get behind."

I open my eyes and simply nod. I don't have much of an option. My world is being turned upside down, but I'd never be able to bounce back from hurting someone. I have no choice but to accept help from the strange man and hope that I don't regret it. "What are you? How did you erase their memories of what I did with a snap?"

"I'm a warlock, the male version of a witch. I come from a line of very powerful witches. But this isn't about me. I need to know more about you so I know how to help. Start from the beginning. Tell me everything that has happened until now that you couldn't explain." He climbs on the metal table and sits next to me as I prepare to share all the craziness that has been my life. Every word that I utter is confirmation that my life will never be the same again.

I give Mr. Blakey the play by play, relieved to be able to get it all off my chest. His eyebrows knit as he hangs on to every word. I pull the bandage off my wrist, and at first, he doesn't speak. He assesses the branding as he skims a lone finger over the elevation.

"And this just appeared three days ago on its own?" he confirms.

"Yes."

"Quite interesting." He inspects closer. "I've never witnessed such a thing."

"What does all this mean?"

"To be honest, I'm not sure. I will need to acquire the help of my trusted colleagues, but we'll get to the bottom of it."

He scoots off the table and then reaches for my hand. I let him help me down. The soreness is noticeably gone. "Where are you taking me?" I ask. He begins to walk toward the door without releasing my hand.

"To the academy." His stride never breaks.

"But I thought you just said I can't go until you were sure that I was stable and not a threat to the other students. And why is my pain suddenly gone?"

I stop so he is forced to as well. He turns and look at me, probably annoyed, but I have so many more questions.

"We have no choice. From the things you just shared, I'm almost certain that you're not any of the supernatural beings that exists here on this Earth. And if I'm right, you're in more danger than I initially thought."

He begins to walk again, and this time, I let him lead me. When we step outside into a wooded area, I'm tempted to fire more questions at him, but I hold them for now. We walk for approximately forty minutes before we come to an open clearing. Before us, a wrought iron gate opens. Lush greenery stretches out as far as the eye can see with medieval, cathedral-like buildings in the distance. The architecture is astoundingly beautiful.

"Is this it? The academy?" I ask in awe.

"Sure is. You'll be safe here. The entire campus is veiled— from both humans and other supernatural beings. That means only students, faculty, and authorized personnel can see or find it."

"Where are we? Because I'm pretty sure there aren't

medieval-like buildings in the middle of Seattle or even Washington for that matter."

"You'd be incorrect. We're not far actually. We're in Snoqualmie Falls, which is about twenty-nine miles east of Seattle. We're on sacred tribal ground, so this land is off-limits to the public without an invitation. And since the entire institution and its grounds are cloaked from visibility, it's a safe place."

"And the medieval part?"

"Our academy was constructed for a sense of nobility, but its infrastructure also binds with our magic to help keep it hidden. It allows natural light in from the sun while refracting the accompanying UV rays that would otherwise be harmful to our vampire students. And now that we've had our little history lesson of the academy, I see that Miranda has arrived."

A middle-aged, raven-haired woman walks up to greet us. "Randolph." A knowing look passes between them before she gives me a warm smile. "Give us a second, dear," she says politely before pulling him to the side.

I can't make out what they're saying, but I'm distracted by the students in the near distance. The scene really does look like any other college campus with the exception of the unique exterior. Would I fit in here? How long before I can return to my own university? A week? One thing is for certain; the sooner, the better. I can't allow myself to get behind.

"Thank you for your patience, Genesis. I'm Professor

Winters. <u>Mr. Blakey</u> has me caught up to speed on your situation," the woman greets as he begins to walk away.

"Nice to meet you," I reply.

"You as well. You're in good hands here. Follow me and we'll go over a few things before we get you situated."

I go to wave goodbye to <u>Mr. Blakey,</u> but he doesn't turn around, so I follow the raven-haired woman. That's all I seem to do lately—blindly follow people. We pass several students, who all seem normal enough. But they couldn't be if they were here, right?

"Define normal, dear," Professor Winters challenges as she gestures for me to enter what looks to be an office.

"Gah, I keep forgetting you people can read minds. Not to be rude, I just wish everyone would stay out of my head."

"*You people?* You're one of us now. This is your normal —our normal. Having supernatural abilities doesn't mean that we're inferior."

I take a seat in a Queen Ann chair near an unlit fireplace. I study the plethora of ancient looking books on shelves that stretch from wall to wall. Anything to avoid eye contact with the woman who has just put me in my place. I didn't mean to sound judgmental, but they were my personal thoughts. It's not like I said it out loud.

"We manifest the things in our thoughts. I take no offense. This is all new to you, and you have a lot to learn. Can I get you some tea?"

She is reading my thoughts yet again. I simply nod. She brings over a tray with tea, milk, and sugar. She takes hers without the additives and then sits across from me. I add milk and a packet of sugar to mine as she begins her explanation for the reason she's brought me here.

"I'll start by saying that I'm a witch. This academy has been around for about thirty years. The original academy was built in Ireland, and the architecture carried over here in the States. Its building material serves a purpose as well."

"Yes, Mr. Blakey told me. I know this is a school for the supernatural to learn to control their powers, but is it like a regular school too? I'm a senior at my university, and I want to graduate on time without transferring here."

I take a sip of my tea, bracing myself for her answer.

"We're not a regular institution, dear. That means we can't be accredited through regular means. As far as the public is concerned, we don't exist."

"Well, how do the attending students get an education?"

"I never said that we didn't educate our students ... only that we're not accredited. You can't get a traditional degree from our academy." She takes a few sips of her tea before she continues. "Unfortunately, like you, supernatural abilities manifest at different ages. This campus has an age cap of eighteen and up. Our younger students attend our primary campus in Dublin where other supernatural beings are less populated. They are taught only what they can handle, and as they peak in maturity and age, they transition to this campus for advanced studies."

"So basically, all of the students here are advanced?" I

ask wearily. "I definitely won't fit in. I should be at the other school with the beginners. Not that I want to travel to Dublin or anything."

"That wouldn't be an option, I'm afraid. You're too old. Besides, it's not about fitting in. It's about self-discovery and learning to control your abilities. We all have something to learn here. The students get a regular education as you would at any other university, just with supernatural specific academia woven into the schedule. You can increase your course load after passing the fundamentals. Your curriculum will be structured to your needs, so don't worry about what classes you peers are taking."

"But what about my real classes at the University of Washington? I need to know how they will fit in the scheme of things."

"You're not a prisoner. If you decide not to enroll here, you're on your own and subject to the consequences of your uncontrolled and unconditioned abilities. Ignorance won't be accepted as an excuse, and we will not be able to save you. However, if you choose to enroll and learn from us, we will provide an undeniable excuse to the university on your behalf and get permission for you to be transferred to online classes. If you work hard enough, you can earn off-campus privileges as well."

"What's that?" My ears perk up at that. It's the first silver lining in all of this mess.

"Well, as I stated before, our students aren't prisoners here. Once a student shows maturity and accountability with their abilities, they are able to request time away—

whether it be a day pass, weekend pass, or even an extended vacation, depending on their course load. Upon approval, that student is granted a special object that acts as a compass to be able to find their way back here."

"This all so much to remember. I'd be lying if I said I wasn't overwhelmed." I sip on my tea. Online classes don't offer the same experience, but what else can I do? I can't do this on my own.

"And you don't have to, dear." The professor smiles. "That is the whole point of this academy. I'll get you enrolled, and we can talk more later. You've had quite a day, and I don't want to overwhelm you any more than you already are. We can discuss your classification later."

"Wait. Does that mean you know what kind of super-natural being I am?" I ask, surprised.

"I'm almost certain, but I don't know for sure. We have distinctive ways to narrow down a class, and thus far, I've been able to rule them all out. This brings about new possibilities not found currently on Earth, but I have one specific class in mind. I won't discuss it now on the off chance that I'm wrong. Your DNA will confirm if I'm right. Until then, let's get you to your new room."

She gets up so I stand as well. "And when will you get my DNA? The sooner I know what's going on with me, the better."

"I already have it." She smiles, waving the nearly empty tea cup that I left on the tray. "Now let's get you settled."

Patience has never been my strong suit, but the

answers I seek are at the mercy of Professor Winters. I know I should embrace this reprieve before my life changes forever. What happens after I find out? What do I tell Jan and Steve? Will I ever get married or have children if I'm only half human? So much hangs in the balance. This all feels like a bad dream, one that I'm hoping I wake up from in my dorm room. The professor pats me on the shoulder before walking over to a desk in the corner to make a call. Undoubtedly, she was reading my thoughts again, but for once, she chose not to comment on my internal monologue. I listen as she speaks with someone about coming to take me to my new room. I don't hear much else. My own sordid thoughts are too loud.

CHAPTER FOUR

Elysian

"He's not a werewolf," a voice whisper hisses in the near distance. "There is no distinct smell. Well, other than dried sweat of an athlete."

"Maybe he has yet to transition for the first time," the other voice challenges. "What else could he be? His core body temp is 109 degrees."

My eyes struggle to focus. I recognize the white-haired man's voice, but their conversation isn't making any sense. Why are they discussing werewolves? Where am I, and how did we get here? That flash of light that struck us hurt like a bitch. I can barely move, though my head hurts worse than my body.

"You weren't supposed to bring him directly here, Bishop. We have protocols in place for a reason. You were supposed to take him to the clinic first to identify what he is and whether he's stable."

"I know that, Randolph. In my haste to get us out of

there as fast as possible, I teleported us here without thinking." There is a brief pause between the two men before the white-haired man who I now know as Bishop begins to speak again. "He's coming to. Let's get him cooled down. His temp could very well be from the stress of the teleport. Maybe I'm wrong."

I feel hands grab my wrist and turn it over. "I recognize this brand. A young woman I brought here earlier today had the same infinity symbol embedded into her left wrist in the same spot. This can't be a coincidence."

My eyes flutter open as I take in the two men standing over me. I try to move, but a jolt of pain runs down my spine, and an involuntary groan slips past my lips.

"Easy there, son," Bishop warns as he helps me sit up from the sofa I was lying on. "Where did you get this brand?" he asks, pointing at my left wrist.

"I don't know," I grumble. I'm the one who needs to be asking the questions here. "Where am I, and what the hell was that light?"

My head throbs as I try to bring everything into focus.

"You're at the Legion of Supernatural Academy, Elysian. That light you experienced was teleportation. You're safe here in Snoqualmie Falls," Bishop assures.

"I've never heard of Snoqual whatever. Are we still in Pennsylvania?"

"No. We're in Washington, not far from Seattle," the blond dude known as Randolph corrects.

"How is that even possible?" Things are getting weirder by the second. Add in all the insane things that have been happening to me, and I think I may be losing my mind. None of this can be real. I close my eyes and count to ten before opening them again. The two men are still standing over me.

"This is very much real," Randolph says.

"Man, stay out of my head. Both of you," I yell a little too loudly. "Aargh." I wince in pain, rubbing my temples in agony.

"Here, let me help," Randolph offers.

His hands replace mine at my temple. I'm about to knock his hand away as he begins some sort of chant mumbo jumbo. But I can feel the pain begin to dissipate. Whatever he's doing is working because even the soreness in body is gone. How did he do that?

"I'm a warlock," he answers. "We both are."

"A war what?" I ask, ignoring that he is once again reading my thoughts.

"Warlock. It's the male version of a witch."

I scoot back on the sofa, trying to put some distance between us.

"You have nothing to fear from us," Bishop says. "I'm Professor Bishop Guenther, and this is Randolph Blakey, the headmaster of the academy."

"Yeah. I got the Bishop and Randolph bit when you two were discussing werewolves. Do they actually exist too? You think I'm one?"

I don't want to believe any of this is real, but how else do I explain the increased speed and strength. Wait, but how does the fire play into all of this?

"What fire?" Bishop asks.

"Can you please stop with the mind reading thing? It's freaking me out," I admit.

"I don't think you're a werewolf, Elysian. And yes, they do exist. Your core body temp is too high to sustain human life, so you're definitely a supernatural being. We just need to determine what kind."

"Are you saying that I'm not human? I heard you saying something about my body temp being 109 degrees. Isn't it a medical emergency for a temp of 104 or 105?"

"For a human, yes. You're at least half human; it's the other half that we're trying to figure out," Bishop explains.

"Are you two human?"

"Very much so," Randolph confirms. "All supernatural beings found on this Earth are either human or half human just with enhanced abilities—well, with the exception of vampires who are immortal."

"So I'm either a warlock or a werewolf, and since you've seemed to rule out werewolf, I must be a warlock like the two of you," I deduce.

"No," Randolph interrupts. "Our body temps don't run as high as yours. My theory is that you're something else. Something that we don't have here on Earth yet. I rescued a young lady earlier today under similar circumstances, and she has the same infinity symbol on her left wrist as you do."

This really gets my attention. "What similar circumstances?"

"She unleashed her supernatural abilities without trying in a room full of humans, which is against the rules. This use of power sent out a beacon to other supernatural beings outside this academy. Two shapeshifters had already come to investigate when I intervened and teleported her to a safe place. You weren't supposed to come here first until we knew what we were dealing with."

"But he's here now," Bishop points out.

"Yes. I'm less guarded now that I see you have similarities with the girl. Her classification is also unknown, but the two of you are connected somehow. I've heard how her powers first began to manifest, so why don't you tell me about anything that you haven't been able to explain so I can look for similarities," Randolph says.

I start from the beginning. I tell him about my dream of shooting fire from my hands and waking up with my apartment on fire. I tell him about the impossible weight that I was able to lift, the speed at which I arrived to class on time, and then finally, the brand that I just noticed on my wrist today. I don't know how any of this is possible, but I'm not sure I want to find out. I keep hoping that I'm back on my buddy's sofa having a nightmare and just haven't woke up yet.

"From your recollection of the odd events, the only similarity the two of you have is the infinity brand. We need more info, but I'm certain that your classification results will be the same. Meaning whatever supernatural being she is, you are too," Randolph explains.

He looks over at Bishop. "Miranda thinks she has an

idea. She has the girl's DNA and is currently working to confirm her suspicion."

"What other supernatural beings are there? You listed four," I inquire. "Witches, warlocks, vampires, and werewolves."

"Those are the ones found on Earth. You got them all correct except for the werewolves. The last one is shapeshifters. Werewolves aren't the only breed of that class. There are other shapeshifters here beside wolves," Randolph corrects. "As far as what other supernatural beings there are, you'll learn that later with your studies. We will focus first on what occupies Earth."

"Wait … what studies? I know you mentioned this is an academy, but I can't stay here. I have a full course load at Penn State and wrestling season to get ready for."

The two men look at each other with weary lines etched in their foreheads.

"Elysian," Bishop begins. "You can't go back to your old life like this. We have to first identify your class and then help you control your abilities. This is what the academy is for. If you leave now, not only are you in danger because the other supernatural beings won't stop until they eliminate you, but you also risk hurting someone else."

"I don't accept this. None of this. I didn't ask for any of it."

"I know," Randolph speaks. "But what happens when you're wrestling an opponent and your uncontrolled abilities set this kid on fire? Better yet, how could you, in good conscience, wrestle another student, knowing that your enhanced abilities are tipping the scale in your favor? It's the equivalent of taking steroids, and it's cheating. And when they test you, pesky things like your 109-degree body temp are going to draw suspicion. And that's if you're not found first and killed by other supernatural beings out there."

"Okay, I get it. Goddammit!" I growl. I know they're both right, but it isn't fair. I work my ass off to get good grades and make my parents proud. I work my ass off in the gym to give my wrestling team my best. I don't want this life. What do I tell my parents ... my girl? Well, ex-girl, but I haven't given up on winning her back.

"Watch your language, son. We can help you transfer to online classes at your university so that you don't get behind academically. You'll have to think of something to tell your team, though. Our students do get privileges to leave campus, but it has to be earned. We have to know that your abilities are under control and that you're mature enough to use them responsibly and follow the rules," Bishop mentions.

"And how long does that take?" I ask, refraining from more profanity.

"That depends on you and your discipline to learn," Randolph says. "I have to get going to meet up with Miranda, but hopefully, I'll see you soon."

He leaves the office without a backward glance.

"What did he mean hopefully?"

"You're not a prisoner here, Elysian. The students we have are here on their own free will."

Bishop explains that students under the age of eighteen attend their academy located in Dublin. They are enrolled by their parents once it's discovered they have supernatural abilities. This campus is for eighteen and up. Even though it's for advanced studies, I was brought here because of my age. I'm considered an adult, so I have to consent to being here. If I don't, then I'm on my own. I will be subject to face any consequences for my uncontrolled abilities. This isn't a choice at all. As much as it pangs me, I have to do the right thing. I'll be enrolling here and doing everything within my power to get back to where I belong. When I woke up this morning, I never could have fathomed that this would be the direction my life would take me. I'm walking away from everything that means anything to me.

"I guess it's settled. What other choice do I have?" I mumble. "Just tell me what I have to do to get whatever I am under control."

"Don't feel so defeated, son. We're going to help you. I know all of this is a lot to take in," Bishop says. "First let me show you to your room. Brody will be your roommate, and he'll help get you settled and oriented to the academy."

He gestures for me to follow him, so I do. As we walk the grounds of the campus, I look around in awe. I can definitely see how their Dublin campus must influence the architecture. The medieval-like cathedrals are so out of place here, but it's breathtakingly beautiful.

"These buildings are something else," I say out loud.

"Yeah. It mimics our primary campus in Dublin, but it also binds without magic to keep this place veiled."

"Veiled?"

He explains how the academy is situated on sacred tribal land, but it is veiled with an illusion spell to render it invisible to anyone who isn't a member here. If I wander off campus beyond the allotted borders, I will not be able to find my way back without a special amulet. Even if the campus is right in front of my face. This keeps the students from sneaking off campus without a granted pass. We make it to my dorm room, and I'm surprised at all the space. My side of the room is bare, and the other side is filled with pics of television wrestlers and other memorabilia.

"Brody is a big fan of wrestling. I think the two of you will hit off and have lots to discuss. He's in class at the moment but make yourself comfortable. I'll bring back some basic bedding and necessities to get you started."

"And clothes? What about my stuff?"

"Tomorrow after we get you settled and have more answers, we'll make arrangements for one of the faculty members to retrieve your belongings." He is almost out the door when he turns back around. "Everything is going to be okay. We've all been where you are at some point. Your life will be different now, but you get to decide if you're optimistic or pessimistic. That will be the difference."

He closes the door behind him, and I'm left alone with my thoughts. I stare down at the infinity symbol on my wrist and blow out a frustrated breath. I sit on the bare, full-sized bed, willing myself to find the positive in this, but I can't. What am I? Where will my life go from here? What happened to my backpack? My phone? I need someone to talk to who's from the sane part of my life, but what would I say? I stretch out on the bed and close my eyes. I never take afternoon naps with my busy schedule, but I welcome the reprieve the exhaustion brings. I let my mind shut off for a bit as sleep takes over.

CHAPTER FIVE

Genesis

"I'm Loren," the lithe blonde introduces no sooner than we leave Professor Winter's office. "Did you just transfer from Dublin?"

"Hi. Umm, no. I'm from Seattle. My name is Genesis." I increase my stride to keep up with her. Other than a little too energetic, she seems friendly enough.

"Oh, how cool. Genesis meaning the beginning, like in the Bible?"

Surprised she picked up on the reference, I smile. "You can say that. My folks have a thing for biblical names."

"So what are you?"

"What do you mean?" I know what she is referring to, so why am I stalling?

"What kind of supernatural being are you? I hope you're a vampire." She giggles.

"I'm not sure yet. That's what Professor Winters is

working on. This is all new to me. Three days ago, I was just an ordinary girl with an ordinary life. This is all so crazy—like a nightmare I can't wake up from." Her mouth goes slack. "Anyway, I'm trying not to be a Debbie Downer until I know more. Why are you hoping that I'm a vampire?"

"Because they're badass. And because you're very pretty. Madison is going to be so envious of you. Before you arrived, she has easily been the most coveted girl here. She's a vampire and a conniving twat. Too bad she doesn't hold a candle to you." She giggles again. "The pretty part, not the *twat* part."

"Well, I'm not into childish high school antics and cattiness. I'm not looking to get involved with anyone here. I was just dumped earlier today, and I'm not looking to start anything new with all the craziness that is my life at the moment. I just want to keep my head down and get through this. I have a real university to graduate from."

"Ouch." Loren winces, stopping in front of a door that I'm guessing is to my room. "This academy is just as important as your precious university."

"I didn't mean to offend you. I just meant I have a lot on my plate, and the last thing anyone needs to worry about is me stealing any attention. I want to be invisible."

"Lighten up, red." She grins as she runs a single hand through my ginger red hair. "I'm totally screwing with you. Most of us are taking additional classes online toward a degree outside of this place too. The fact of the matter is, you're the new girl, and you're insanely hot.

Attention is not something you're going to be able to avoid. I'd just advise against the whole *'real university'* remarks."

"Is this me?" I ask, pointing toward the door. She nods, so I turn the knob and enter. The room is bare on one side, which is to be expected. Loren follows me in. I'm too distracted by the gorgeous décor on the other side of the room. My dorm has never looked anything close to this. Lights twinkle along the wall, golden drapes hang from the ceiling to the floor, matching the plush comforter. Chanel Haute Couture fashion pics cover an inspiration board. Everything is so modern and luxurious compared to the historical presence of this building. The interior of the building showcases high ceilings, archways, and a rich history that carries over from the medieval cathedral architecture outside. But not inside this room. It's like we've turned the page and entered another realm in time. I love the contradiction of this décor.

"You like?"

"It's gorgeous. My roommate must be swimming in money—well, have parents who are. I don't even know what designer that bedding is, but I just want to touch it."

"It's Michael Amini. Go ahead and touch it. I won't tell."

I walk over to the bed and run my hands along the softness. I pick up one of the embroidered pillows. "LB," I read. "Well, I hope she's not some rich snotty brat. Wait ... how do you know what designer this is?" It just occurred to me that she could be rich too. They could all be. "Or was this bedding standard issued from the academy?"

This time, she lets out a hearty laugh. "I'm LB, genius. As in *Loren Blakely*. This is my room too. You're my new roommate."

"Dammit. I've stuck my foot in my mouth again. I should just stop talking."

"It's totally fine. I'm rather enjoying your assumptions. Your face turns so red every time you realize your mistake."

"Wait. *Blakely*, as in Headmaster Blakely?" I ask, putting the pieces together.

"Yep. That is my uncle."

"So why even bother having a roommate? You can have this place all to yourself. Your uncle runs this entire school."

"Because, believe or not, not all people with money are pretentious snobs. Or how did you put it? Some *'rich, snotty brat'*? Having just one roommate is actually a privilege. Some have three or four in a room."

"So sorry, Loren. I promise I'm not some judgmental bitch. Before today, this was all fiction to me, like entertainment to watch on television. I haven't been myself lately, and the stress of it all has me on edge. Let's start over."

"Don't worry, red. You can't push me away that easily. You and I are going to be great friends. I don't go by words. I rely on vibes, and yours is a good one. So as your new roommate and friend, I vow to get you through all of this."

"Thank you." I pull out my phone to show her the incident in the coffee shop. I get a good vibe from her too, so I'm okay with sharing what happened. "This is me accidentally freezing the entire coffee shop," I say as I point my phone in her direction.

"That's just a white screen." She shakes her head. "What is it?"

"I accidentally froze all the people and everything in it," I share.

"That means you froze your phone and all of its components too. I have a lot to teach you."

"Well, there goes proof that it actually happened."

"You don't want proof of your indiscretions. What you did is against the rules. Your eyes are the only proof that you need. You're not crazy. This supernatural existence is very real."

"Your uncle intercepted me before I could be captured by two shapeshifters that were closing in on me."

"As I said, you have a lot to learn, and I have much to teach you. You're at a slight disadvantage because you came straight here instead of learning from an early age as most of us did."

"I figured as much. I've always been at the top of my class—grade wise. Now I get to start at the bottom. I get to see how it feels not to be the smartest in the room."

"Learning about your abilities and how to use them appropriately is not a sprint. Intelligence has nothing to do with it, so you shouldn't compare yourself to anyone. Come on, let's get out of here for a while. I have some people I'd like you to meet."

A knock on the door interrupts us. The door opens without acknowledgment from either of us, and a small gray-haired woman walks through with a blanket, sheet set, pillows, and toiletries. She never utters a single word. She just places the things on my bed and turns to leave. "Thank you," I say anyway. She simply nods before leaving.

"That's Gertrude," Loren informs me. "She normally gets the newbies settled with the essentials until you can get your own. She also ensures that the students in this wing don't break any rules such as cooking in our room, breaking curfew, or sneaking guys in." She laughs.

"So she's similar to the RA or resident assistant we have at our university," I point out.

"I've only ever done online classes, so I'll have to take your word for it," she admits. "Anyway, what do you say about getting out of here for a bit?"

"I'm going to have to pass for today. I'm exhausted, and to be frank, I need a little more time to wrap my head around all of this."

"That's understandable. We have plenty of time to get to know each other and for me to introduce to the cool people," she jokes. "I won't be out too long."

"See you later," I reply, but she is already out the door.

Finally, I get some solitude. I make my bed with the supplied linens and organize my toiletries in our bathroom. This room is definitely nicer than my dorm room at the university. For starters, our shared space isn't this large, and we don't have the luxury of our own bathroom. You carry your shower tote down the hall to shower as a group—very little privacy. My eyes light up when I see the tub. It's a standard tub, but I can't wait to soak in it. It's nice to have something to look forward to. It will have to wait until I get my clothes, I guess, since I don't have anything to change into.

I crawl into bed and try to block out the remaining light. The sun doesn't set until after nine, so we have another hour of daylight. I pull the blanket over my head, surprised at how tired I actually am. I don't think about anything. Instead, I allow myself to give in to the exhaustion.

Two men are chasing me. I can't look back, but I feel them getting closer. They've been sent to kill me. I'm in a forest, and the brush is thick. Twigs snap beneath my feet, giving away my location. I can't run any faster. They're getting closer. I feel one of their hands grab my shoulder, and I let out a piercing scream. This is it. I'm going to die.

"Genesis, wake up," a familiar male voice says. I can feel him shaking me. "Wake up. You're dreaming."

I manage to open my eyes. Breathing heavily, I latch onto him except there is no orb of light this time. I'm still in my bed, and Mr. Blakely is sitting on the side.

Darkness blankets the room. A few more heavy pants leave me.

"Mr. Blakely?" I ask with need for confirmation.

"Yes. You're safe. You were having a nightmare."

"What are you doing here? What made you come?"

"I called him," Loren's voice admits in the near distance. "Don't you feel that?"

"Feel what?" I begin to sit up with Mr. Blakely's help.

"I got this, Loren. Let me handle it. Thank you for your concern and for calling me."

"Can someone tell me what's going on, already?"

I hear a distinct cracking sound before we're bathed in light. Now with the room lights turned on, I freak. I cover my mouth, but a squeal still slips past. The entire room is covered in ice— the walls, the door, the windows, and even the beds.

"When I got back to the room, I noticed how cold the door handle was. The door was frozen from the inside. I called my uncle immediately," Loren explains as I look around the room in fear.

"Did I do this?" Mr. Blakely nods, but I knew the answer before I even asked. It's like the lake thing. I go to bed and wake up to crazy shit happening.

"From what I can tell, this was a response to stress. What were you dreaming about?" he asks.

"The two men you rescued me from were chasing me again, except this time we were in a forest. They wanted to kill me, and I couldn't make myself run any faster. They had nearly caught me before you woke me up."

"Hmmm. And when you froze all those people in that coffee shop, your boyfriend has just broken up with you ... Am I right?"

"Yes. What does this mean?"

"It means stress is your trigger. Your powers are growing. When I leaned into the coffee shop to wipe their memories of what had happened, I did notice a chill to the room, but I contributed it to the air conditioning. I now think that it was a weaker form of your power. You weren't quite able to unleash the ice, but even the weakest of your ability was able to freeze everything in there completely still," Mr. Blakely explains.

"But don't you need water to make ice?" Loren asks, curiously.

"All air has some water vapor in it. That's where we get humidity and condensation from," I answer. "The question is, how do we get rid of it all without creating a river in our room once it all melts?"

Mr. Blakely points at the window that's lifted just enough. "Genesis is correct on how the ice was formed. We're going to raise this window a bit more and send it all out there where it can melt."

Loren wastes no time doing as he says and pushing the screen until it falls to the ground. Thankfully, we're on the first floor so there's nobody for it to fall onto.

Mr. Blakely closes his eyes and arranges his hands midair. He twirls his finger without so much as a single chant. No hocus-pocus, mumbo jumbo at all. Still, I watch in amazement as pieces of ice break and begin to swirl around him. One by one, they form a uniform line out the open window before hitting the ground. This process continues until every bit of the ice is gone. I know I've been reassured several times since I've teleported here with him and have been shown plenty of evidence, but for some reason, this moment solidifies my new reality. *This* is real. *This* just happened.

"Wow! Will I be able to do that? Move stuff with my mind, I mean?"

"I don't know. Maybe. But first we need to teach how to control your abilities. Right now, your stress is in control," Mr. Blakey answers. He gestures for Loren to close the window, and she does. "Try to get some rest. We will retrieve your things from your university, and then you have a day of tests ahead of you."

"What kind of tests?" I ask suspiciously.

"For starters, you will need a physical exam so we can establish a baseline for your health. Then we will put your body through some physical stress in the form of exercise," he informs. "We have a meeting with Miranda at nine to see what she was able to confirm. And just so you know, another student was brought in after you with the same infinity symbol on his wrist. We believe you two are the same. See you at eight a.m. sharp in my office. Loren will escort you."

"But—"

"Good night, Genesis," he interrupts. And just like that, he's gone.

"Your uncle is pretty good at the whole disappearing

act. He drops a bomb in my lap and then vanishes. I have so many questions."

"Yeah. He's direct like that—a straight shooter. He makes his point or says what he feels needs to be said, and then he's done. It's not personal. It's just his way." She pulls me over to sit on the edge of her bed. "Now can we talk about more important things like you being an ice queen."

"Ugh. I'm so sorry. I don't even know how I did it. I still don't know how I can go from being a boring, normal girl to freezing shit. And who is this guy that your uncle speaks of? I wonder if we're related."

"First off, I doubt you were ever boring. Second, I wish I could freeze shit. That's so cool—literally."

"What are your powers?" I can't believe I haven't asked her this before now, but I guess the proverbial ice has been broken.

"My family and I are known as cradle witches. It means that we were born with an affinity for magic and it gets passed down in our lineage. There is so much we can do if we know the right spell. Some things don't require incantation, such as moving objects with our minds as you witnessed my uncle do with the ice."

"What is incantation?"

"It's a series of words or a chant spoken as a spell."

"So is there a class that you take to learn spells or incantations?"

"They teach us some basic stuff, but the more powerful spells are kept in a Grimoire. Think of it as a huge reference book with almost every spell there is. So of course, it's not accessible to us. We learn only what they want us to know."

"So I'm guessing these classes are restricted to witches and warlocks."

"Correct. That's why classification is so important. Your education is tailored to your abilities. Plus, just because you learn a spell doesn't mean you should or could perform it. You have to be physically strong enough to channel all the power you call upon or you can die."

"Holy shit! This is so much more than I originally thought."

"Hey. Don't go getting all stressed out again. We don't want you to make Iceland out of our room again." She giggles, and I can't help but join her.

"I wonder who this mystery guy is?"

"I don't know, but I do know that eight a.m. will come quick. My uncle doesn't do tardiness," she jokes.

"I hate that I'll be stuck wearing the same thing until they can finally get my clothes."

She jumps off the bed and pulls me up. She looks me up and down and smiles. "Easy fix. You can borrow something of mine. We're about the same size—well except for those double d hooters protruding from your chest."

"Hush! I didn't ask for these. Good thing I don't play sports or they'd be much more of a hassle."

"Are you serious?"

"Serious about what?"

"You don't play sports at all? Like ever?"

Her jaw slacks in awe. Then I figure out why she is so shocked. "Don't let the muscularity fool you. It's natural. I don't do crap. Probably in my genes or something. And before you ask, I recently found out I was adopted, and no, I don't know who my biological parents are."

"Oh. I was just going to say you're ripped like someone who lives in the gym. You look like you can kick some serious ass."

I roll my eyes at her because it's nothing I haven't heard before. "Nope. Not even a little bit. I'm not a fighter."

"Well, to change the subject ... you look about a size four. Am I right?"

"Meh. Give or take. My butt sometimes edges me into a bigger size."

"After the reaction I got about your girls, I wasn't going to even mention the butt. We're the same size basically; you just have more curves." She goes over to the dresser and begins to rummage through it. "For now, here is a tank and some shorts so you can take a shower. We'll find you something to wear in the morning. You'll be issued the standard uniform after you've been fitted."

"Thanks," I say as I take the clothes from her outstretched hand.

"No problem. I left you three drawers empty for your stuff once you get it. Plus, you can have half the closet."

CHAPTER SIX

Elysian

I pace in front of the large window overlooking the campus. It's nearly eight a.m. here, which with the time difference means I would have already attended my first two morning classes and be on my way to work out before lunch back home. I couldn't sleep last night with my fate hanging in the balance. Professor Winters and Mr. Blakey are gathered around his desk, looking at some leather-bound book with aged pages. They won't tell me anything until some girl gets here. Apparently, we have something in common that they want to explore, but I just want to get on with it. As if hearing my plea, the door swings open, and two girls appear. The first girl through the door is a green-eyed blonde with a pixie cut and tomboyish mannerisms. The cliché schoolgirl uniform is no match for her swagger.

"The welcome committee has arrived," she sings as

she takes a bow. Mr. Blakey scowls at the interruption. I like this girl already.

That's when I see her. The girl who walks in after the crazy blonde. Her steps are unsure as she looks around the room. Long fire-red hair shields her face from me. Oh, but her body couldn't be hidden even if she tried. Large bountiful breasts strain against her black tank that is a size too small. Her ass to petite waist ratio is completely drool worthy. Rounding off the total package, she's fit—shredded and stacked. I'm a faithful guy, so I'd never go there, but there is not a man alive who wouldn't appreciate her assets. I'm technically single, but I don't have plans to fuck around in the interim of the break with my girl back home.

"Mr. Remis, are you ready to get started?" Mr. Blakey asks, his brow lifted.

"Um, yes," I answer, slightly embarrassed that I got caught checking out the redhead. If I had to guess, I'd say she was the one we were waiting on.

"Then have a seat."

He gestures for us to have a seat on the sofa after he dismisses the blonde. He introduces us, and I learn that her name is Genesis. There is an awkward pause, and I realize my thoughts have drifted again. I look up, expecting him to be giving me "busted" look again, but instead, he is inspecting her wrist. He quickly grabs mine and does the same.

"The infinity symbols ... they're gone. How is that

possible?" he asks, confused. He's right. I hadn't even noticed. When did it disappear?

"I think I have an idea," Professor Winters speaks for the first time. "First let me explain what I've discovered."

"Please," Genesis encourages.

"Using your DNA, I created an identity spell. The gist being that your DNA samples were infused into a potion before being laid out on a roadmap of possible supernatural being prospects. Both DNA samples trekked into the deity space."

"Deity? What does that mean?" I want her to just spit it out. What is she trying to tell us?

"Deities are divine. I'm saying that you're a demigod, and Genesis is a demigoddess," Professor Winters explains.

"So you're telling me that my parents are gods? Demi means half god and half human, right?"

"Are you even listening to yourself?" Genesis snaps. Her glacial eyes are nearly clear. It's both freaky and sexy. I can't help but stare into them as she stands there being a smartass. "She's telling you that your parents aren't your parents. Now it makes sense, knowing I'm adopted, but how could my real parents be gods?"

"You're the one not listening, smartass. Demi means only one parent is a god. The other parent has to be human so that means one of my parents may still be biological. Just because you have adoptive issues ..."

"Alright!" Mr. Blakey yells. "Enough. Both of you. We're here to get answers, not attack each other. There are more important things to focus on here. The two of you are unique on this Earth, and this puts you in danger."

"How is that?" Genesis asks, turning her attention away from me. *Fucking redheads.* What a little spitfire.

"For starters, you don't have the protection of a group. Witches have covens, werewolves have packs, and vampires have clans. Seeing as the two of you are the only ones of your kind here on Earth, you only have each other. Which brings me to my next point."

Professor Winters walks up behind me and places her fingertips at my temple. She chants some two-syllable word repeatedly. Genesis immediately doubles over, crying out in agony. She walks over to her and repeats the process. I brace myself to feel whatever pain she inflicted on Genesis, but nothing. Oddly enough, her cries stop even though the professor is inflicting her magic directly.

"I don't feel the pain anymore," Genesis confirms as she sits up straight.

The professor and Mr. Blakey look back and forth between each other.

"Why did Genesis feel pain when you did your juju to me but not when you did it to her? And why didn't I feel anything either time?"

"That wasn't juju, Elysian. That word is derived from evil," Professor Winters chastises. "The two of you are connected. You feel what is being done to the other, but you're the stronger one. When I was inflicting pain on you, she absorbed all of your pain. Felt everything in your place. When the roles were reversed, she didn't feel anything because you were absorbing her pain. Only your pain threshold is higher, so it wasn't enough to make you notice."

"Holy shit! This is crazy."

"Language," Professor Winters and Mr. Blakey warn simultaneously. I look over at Genesis; her eyes are wide with disbelief.

"Could we be related? Same parent?" she asks.

"No. Your DNA ruled that out. But there's more. I've studied a bit about quantum entanglement. It starts with a simple connectivity and continues to build into inevitable entanglement. Once the quantum entanglement is complete, you'd be like two halves of a whole—absorbing and sensing each other's energy. I don't know why you both have the infinity symbol, but it's your link to each other. You were meant to find each other, and I think the branding is a form of magnetic energy that pulls you two together. Now that you're in the same place, it fades under the surface."

"So if we're a great distance apart, then it would reappear?" I ask, confused.

"Exactly."

"Why are we the only two?" I ask.

"That's a good question, and one I'm afraid I can't answer today." She looks over at Mr. Blakey. "As I said before, being the only two makes you vulnerable. Outside of this school are supernatural beings that would seek to harm or even eliminate you if they find out what you are."

"But why? You just said there are only two of us. We're not a threat."

"It has to do with hierarchy. I said you two were vulnerable. I never said you were weak. Deities are more powerful than anything that walk this Earth. Once you learn to harness and control your powers, you will be a threat and even more so as that power strengthens. So you can see why some would find it advantageous to eliminate you before you reach that pinnacle."

"Great! So not only am I some demigoddess, but I'm also a threat to all supernatural beings that walk the Earth. I can see the line forming now to knock us down a peg or two."

"So don't tell them," I suggest in reference to the other students. "I have to agree. We're already the new kids on the block, so this just places a monumental target on our backs."

"We don't exactly have a curriculum for you since you're the first of your class. A program will have to be customized for you, which may incite suspicion from your peers," Mr. Blakey points out.

"Well, not necessarily," Professor Winters challenges. "They'll both start with the general courses that are the foundation for every student. From there, the different course load can be explained away by them explaining they haven't advanced to the more difficult courses yet. Since most students transfer from our Dublin campus, it isn't a stretch."

"The choice will be yours whether to share your classification with your peers, but I can see how a lie or omission would quickly become daunting and lead to mistrust. I have to get going, but Miranda will explain the next step." He gives a simple nod before leaving.

"Randolph has a point. But this is a lot to take in. Take a few days to process all that we've told you, and then make the decision together."

"So what's next?" Genesis asks, changing the subject.

"Well, from our collective baseline assessments, you have the power of glaciokinesis, and Elysian has the power of ignikinesis."

"English, please," I joke.

"Ice and fire manipulation," she clarifies. "But Elysian, you also reported increased strength and speed. Genesis, you reported unconscious teleportation to a lake. Today, we're going to work on finding out what your individual powers are so that we have a baseline for your studies and training. I don't promise that we will uncover all of your abilities as some may not be available yet."

"How can some of our abilities not be available yet?" I ask.

"Some powers lay dormant and can only be brought forth with increased knowledge and mental readiness. Using our powers requires a lot of energy, and if our minds and bodies are not conditioned to handle it, we can cause harm to ourselves. So if abilities remain in a dormant state, it's often to protect us from ourselves."

"I guess I'm as ready as I'll ever be," Genesis admits.

"Same," I agree.

"Good. I'll be the one working with you today, and based on our findings, I'll create a specialized curriculum in addition to your general studies. For now, let's head to our identification lab. It's where we can safely try to lure out your powers." She laughs.

I can't believe she just made a joke. It's the first relatable side I've seen from her thus far. Between her, Mr. Blakey, and Professor Guenther, they are all too serious. Freaking mind readers that answer all your questions before you get a chance to ask. If I'm being honest, it's nice to have someone to endure all of this with—even if she is insanely hot with a smart mouth.

CHAPTER SEVEN

Genesis

I've been running on this treadmill for the last fifteen minutes, yet it feels like I've ran a marathon—not that I've actually attempted one. Beads of sweat run down my forehead and chest. My chest heaves, and my throat becomes increasingly dry as I fight for each breath. Still, I maintain my composure and form as the programmed machine increases the speed yet again. It's set to increase every five minutes. A red light on the display dash blinks to warn me of the increase. The only motivation I'm holding on to is the fear of falling flat on my face in front of the ridiculously handsome guy who I'm apparently connected with. He couldn't be more beautiful if he tried. Gorgeous cerulean blue eyes, a chiseled face worthy of a god, a dimpled chin, and a muscular physique that is impossible to ignore. He has tattoo sleeves on both arms and his left chest that gives him the edge of a bad boy, except they're Disney, Christmas, and

God related— as in the man upstairs. He's an enigma for sure. I watch as he powerfully makes strides next to me, his breathing even. Normally, I'm not attracted to the jock types, but I'd be lying if I said my heart didn't quiver at the sight of him. Too bad he comes off as a douche know-it-all with little regard for authority.

I'm so deep into my internal monologue that I miss the warning of the next speed increase and lose my rhythm and footing. My hands flail out in front of me, crushing all hope of saving face. I unleash some sort of *stresscicle* and turn the entire treadmill into a block of ice, which then sends me flying backward. I brace for impact with the ground, but strong muscular arms catch me. Elysian's swift movements were a blur. My embarrassment was momentarily distracted by his superhuman speed. He was running alongside me, yet he had time to both react and catch me before my ass hit the floor. I take back what I said about him being a douche know-it-all.

"Wow! I'm impressed," Professor Winters admits as she appears from behind the glass office. "Elysian, I do believe we just witnessed one of your abilities in action."

"Thank you," I say politely as he helps me back to my feet.

"Of course." He smirks. And just like that, my original opinion of him returns exponentially.

"Impeccable timing to take out this," Professor Winters states, pulling a probe thing from her lab jacket. My eyes widen. "Relax, it's just to take your temperatures."

She slides the wand-like probe over my temple and then repeats for Elysian. She heads back to the small office behind the glass, so we follow her.

"What does our temperatures tell you?" I ask as she records her findings onto a clipboard.

"Well Genesis, your temp is 93 degrees, yet you show no signs of hypothermia. Elysian is on the other side of the spectrum. His temp is 109, which ordinarily would be hyperthermia. Neither of you have temps sustainable with human life, yet you're both standing here unaffected."

"She didn't feel that cold to me," Elysian says.

"That's because you're so hot," the Professor explains. I snicker. "Your body temp is hot, so it absorbs your ability to feel how cold she is," she corrects, after realizing it sounds like she was saying he was hot. *Which he is.*

"So we've learned that stress is the trigger to accidental use of your powers. And your body temperatures may be a correlation to the stress. Your baseline temperatures were both 98.6, which is the normal temp for a human. Your stress responses or when your powers are at play drive your temps in opposite directions. I'll record the parameters of the treadmill that invoked that stress response," she says, eyeing me. I wonder if she knows my *"stress response"* was more likely from getting ready to face plant in front of the handsome jackass and not the actual speed increase.

She nods in the affirmative, and I wish the floor could swallow me whole. Of course, she knows. She's probably been reading my thoughts this entire time. She's helping me save face in front of Elysian. She takes our other vital signs to ensure that we're stable.

"Why don't the two of you take a break while I get someone to defrost the treadmill?" she suggests.

"Do we have to stay here?" Elysian asks.

"No. Genesis, your belongings should be in your room by now if you want to check. Elysian, your things are being driven down, so give it another day or so."

"Two days? After giving my buddy's address, I thought someone would just teleport it all here. What about my motorcycle?"

"Don't be dense. They can't just bewitch all your stuff here like *I Dream of Jeannie,*" I chastise.

"First of all, that's two different TV shows. Second, nobody asked you. Easy for you to say because your stuff is probably waiting in your room."

"Now, now kids," the professor warns. "It's within our ability to teleport it all here, but it's also against the rules. We can't use magic or our abilities for personal gain. If caught, it's a punishable offense, so you would do well to remember that. You'll learn all about the rules in your first class. For now, we will transport Elysian's belongings here the old-fashioned *human* way."

"So I guess making an ATM give me a limitless amount of money to buy myself a mansion is out of the question," Elysian jokes. I roll my eyes so hard I'm surprised they don't get stuck.

"Now you're catching on," the professor agrees. "Now get going. You only have an hour."

I leave first, and the muscular douche follows. "Ummm, what are you doing?" I finally ask when it's clear he's not traveling in a separate direction.

"Following you."

"I guessed as much, but why?"

"So far, you're the only person I know here, and since it's pointless to head to my room without my stuff being here, I thought I'd go with you to check on yours. Afterward, we can grab a bite to eat …"

"Are you always this forward? Like inviting yourself to do stuff with people?"

"Are you always this bitchy, or is that a side effect your superpower?" He smirks.

I stop in the middle of the sidewalk. "I'm not bitchy. You just ask stupid questions and act like a know-it-all," I accuse.

"You don't know anything about me, sweetheart. But your talons have been out for me from the moment you laid eyes on me. Even after I saved your ass from hitting the floor, you had something snarky to say about me being dense. I'm trying to process all of this just like you. You're not the only one feeling out of sorts and unsure about what this means for your future."

I'm stunned silent. He's right. I've never been the one to lay into people. I'm more of a bite my tongue and ignore you kind of girl. I can admit that I've been just a bit rude. Okay, maybe a lot.

"Look. You're right. I'm stressed as evidenced by my turning shit into ice, but I shouldn't be taking out my frustrations on you. You haven't done anything to me. I apologize."

"You're forgiven. It looks like we're in this together so let's start over. Hi. I'm Elysian Remis, and I love both *Bewitched* and *I Dream of Jeannie*."

I double over in laughter. I love how he slid those old 70s sitcoms back at me. "Hi. I'm Genesis Aldaine, and I love all the Nick at Nite old shows."

"We're going to get along just fine, Ms. Aldaine, because so do I."

I guess he isn't so bad. We walk side by side, discussing all our favorite shows. He tells me about wrestling and his studies at Penn State. He is surprised to learn that I spend absolutely zero time in the gym but not surprised about the book nerd part. He jokingly calls me an overachiever, and I can't disagree. Before long, we're at my dorm room. The door swings open before I can reach for the handle.

"Oh hi," Loren greets as she looks back and forth between us. "Your stuff is here. I just put the TV in the corner and all your other stuff on the bed so you can organize where you want to put it all."

Elysian gives her a small wave. They formally introduce themselves while I stand there awkwardly.

"Where are the good places to eat around here?" he asks.

"I was heading out for a bite myself. I can show you unless you two had other plans," she says, not conspicuously at all.

"No. We only came to see if my things were here. We have to be back within the hour, so food sounds good," I assure.

If she was feeling Elysian, I wasn't going to stand in her way. Hopefully, I made it clear that she had the green light.

"Great. Let's go."

She leads the way, giving us a tour as we walk. Every aspect of this campus is a phenomenal contradiction to the city itself. The columns and archways are a beautiful sight to behold. I plan to explore the grounds more when I get the time.

"I'm down for sure," I hear Elysian comment.

"What about you?" Loren asks, looking at me.

"What about me?" I ask, confused.

"We were talking about the party tonight. It's Friday, so you can usually find something going on around campus. Tonight, Madison is throwing a party in the west wing. It's one of our hangout spots."

"Isn't she the one you were warning me about? I believe your exact words was that she was a *conniving twat*," I recall.

"Yeah, but we're not going to the party for her. It'll be a great chance for you and Elysian to meet some of the other students," Loren explains. "Besides, you already turned down a chance to hang last night."

"Fine. I'm not really a huge partier, but I guess it can't hurt to meet people. It's going to take time to adjust to all of this as my new norm."

"My thoughts exactly," Elysian chimes in. "We might as well embrace this change as much as we can."

We arrive at the main cafeteria. There is a salad bar on one side of the room, a grill for fast type food, and a station with the meal of the day.

"Salad it is," I say.

"The food is actually pretty good here," Loren assures. "Their mushroom burgers are the best, but the beef stroganoff they're serving at the main station is decent too."

"I'm vegetarian," I point out.

"You are?" Elysian asks, surprised.

"Well, I'm sure they have other options. They're pretty inclusive here to the student's dietary needs. I just never noticed those options because I'm all about the beef." Loren grins.

"Hi, Loren. Who are your new friends?" a petite brunette asks.

"Hi. I'm Elysian," he introduces.

Of course, he would be the first to speak up. She's gorgeous. Her perky breasts threaten to make an appearance outside of her white button-down shirt, tied at the waist, her blue plaid skirt barely hitting mid-thigh, and matching knee-high socks complete her ensemble. It's the most obscene school uniform I've ever seen ... Well, the way she wears it is obscene. The same uniform looks normal on Loren. All this chick is missing is the pigtails to her chest-length straight hair to complete her porn style. She bats her whiskey-colored eyes in Elysian's direction, not even trying to hide her flirtation.

"I'm Madison," she replies.

"So you're the one hosting the party tonight?" Elysian smiles.

"Oh, you've heard about it? Great! I hope that means you're coming."

"I'm Genesis," I interrupt.

I'm certain she couldn't care less. Her focus is on the stud I'm entangled with, and I can't say that I blame her. Girls like me never get guys like him, so I don't even try. I'd rather see Loren end up with him, though. Hell, he may not even be single. He's probably a player back home, or he has somebody. I'm sure he has his pick of women.

"Yes. Genesis and I are new here. We'll both be there tonight. Looking forward to meeting some people."

"For sure," she says as she peruses me. "Are you two together? As in a couple?"

"Uh, no. We just met. I'm on a break with someone back home," he clarifies.

"What did you do?" Madison winks.

"That's kind of personal, Madison. Give the guy a break," Loren warns.

"Why do people always assume it's the guy?" Elysian asks. "Shelby and I have been together since our freshman year. She decided we needed to see other people to make sure we were not just settling because we were comfortable with one another. I disagreed, but what could I do?"

That bit of information surprises me. That definitely

sounds like something a guy would suggest and not the other way around. Doesn't seem like he is in a hurry to move on. But you wouldn't get that from the gleam in Madison's eyes. She smiles up at him like it's the best thing she's heard.

"Well, you're technically single, and it's her loss," Madison replies, insensitively. "I look forward to seeing you tonight. Nice meeting you, Janet," she says as an afterthought. None of us bother to correct her.

She walks away, and I'm sure the sway to her hips is for added effect. This is the second time today that I nearly roll my eyes out of my head. She couldn't even get my name right.

"Now you see what I was talking about," Loren says.

"I'm going to grab a salad," I announce. I don't want to give her another thought.

"Okay. Can you grab us a table since you'll probably have your food first?"

"Sure." We nod and agree to meet after we get our food.

I don't know why I'm so disturbed by Madison. I've met my share of Madisons in my lifetime—the popular attention hogs who always get the guy. I need to just keep my head down, find a way to get through this supernatural crap, and graduate. The last time I looked up from my studies and tried to date, Cooper happened. He was an artistic, creative type and caught my attention. The moment he tried to fit in with the jocks and push for us to do more things with that crowd, we begin to drift apart. That wasn't my world. I didn't judge them, but it didn't stop them from judging me. I have no plans to make that mistake again. Loren seems cool enough, but I can't lose focus on my goals. This school is just a pit stop in my journey.

I assemble my salad in no time. I grab a water and head for the register. Surprisingly, Elysian is already in line.

"That was quick," I say.

"Yeah. The main station had a salmon and veggies option if you didn't want the stroganoff. It was a short line since most opted for the grill."

"Lucky you," I joke.

We pay for our food with our smart phones and find a table.

"So tell me more about you," Elysian says, catching me off guard.

"Oh, good. You guys found a table. I wasn't sure there'd be any left," Loren surmises as she sits down with her burger and fries. She begins to discuss the party tonight, so for now, Elysian's question is tabled. I'm grateful for the reprieve.

CHAPTER EIGHT

Elysian

Alternative rock music thumps beneath my feet as a crowd of people swarm around me. Loren introduced Genesis and me to numerous people whose names I've already forgotten before they disappeared to the ladies' room. That was at least twenty minutes ago. I continue to mingle and sip on the alcoholic concoctions being served on the down low. This party is unregulated, but I'm sure open consumption of alcohol on campus isn't allowed.

"There you are. You came," Madison says, appearing out of nowhere.

"Hi. Yeah. Wouldn't miss it."

"Meeting all the classes, I'm assuming?"

"Classes?"

She inches closer, pressing her breast against my arm. Her spandex dress leaves little to the imagination. I know her type well. Underneath all the makeup and sexual attire, she may actually be a great girl, but that's not what she puts forward. Instead, you see someone who is temporary fun.

"Classification," she explains. "I'm a vampire, so that's my class. Most of us are open to other classes, but there are definitely some who are skeptical of anyone outside their own class."

"How can you tell what anyone is. Everyone looks ... you know, normal."

"Because we are normal. Just our own twisted version of it," she jokes. "You'll learn the distinctions. The werewolves are normally warmer to the touch and have a distinctive smell. They don't stink, but it's different. Vampires, witches, and warlocks are little harder to distinguish. When they use their abilities, you can tell them apart."

"And what are your abilities?"

"I'm still learning. We all are. We share some common abilities such as speed and strength, but vampires can also compel humans to do just about anything."

"Hmmm."

"So you never answered my question. What are you? I can feel that your body is warmer than average, but you're missing the smell."

"They're still trying to figure it out," I reply, remembering our discussion earlier today with Professor Winters and Mr. Blakey. I'm not ready to share what I'm still processing myself.

"I'm sure they'll figure it out soon. The faculty here is

so much more advanced with their abilities. At least you've already made one friend—me. Well, besides Loren and Janet."

"Genesis," I correct.

"Whatever. I think she secretly likes you, and that doesn't work for me."

This gets my attention. "Why not?"

She loops an arm through mine. "Let's get another drink. I've said too much already."

I begrudgingly let her off the hook. We grab another drink before she leads me away from the party.

"Where are you taking me?" I question.

"It was getting a little stuffy in there. Just thought I'd show you around. You don't have to be scared."

"Scared isn't the word I'd use. Suspicious, maybe?"

Her mouth gapes open in mock awe. "What are you suspicious about?"

"Your intentions. I think you just wanted to get me alone." I chuckle.

"Guilty. You got me," she admits. "I find you interesting, and I wanted you all to myself. You know ... before all the other women try to get their hooks in you."

"You're honest and direct—I'll give you that—but I'm not looking for anything. I just had my heart shitted on not that long ago. I'm treading with caution."

"I get that. I've only ever given my heart to a guy once. Once he knew how much I cared, he used me and then dump me. Now I'm all about fun. If you don't invest your heart, you can't get hurt."

It's brief, but I see it. The moment she lets her guard down. The slip in her persona. If I had to guess, I'd say the provocative clothing and the "fun" approach with guys was all an act to guard her heart.

"You can't be afraid to put yourself out there over one asshole. The person meant for you will find you, and when they do, you have to be willing to open your heart again."

We walk side by side under the moonlight. She bumps her shoulder just below mine.

"You're pretty cool, you know that? I wouldn't have taken you for such a sensitive guy."

"I wouldn't say sensitive per se but more of a realist. I think we know what the right thing to do is or what's real, but our instinct is to create a more palatable version of the truth. I'm guilty of this as well, but I try to always be as realistic as I can."

"Want to see something cool?" she asks, changing the subject.

"Sure."

The words are barely out of my mouth before a gust of wind whips around me, a blur of her red dress barely visible. Suddenly, Madison is touching my shoulder from behind.

"What the hell was that?" I ask, amazed.

"Me. I made a lap around the school."

"Holy shit. That was fast. I didn't see you leave or come back, but I felt you. I know I have speed too, but I don't know how to activate it."

"Come on. I'll show you. Hold my hand."

"I don't think I can run that fast," I admit.

"It's called dashing and don't worry. Just don't think about it. Clear your mind and just start running. I'll keep pace with you with little boosts if I think you can go faster."

I can't help but grin at her. This is a challenge I'm willing to accept. It's nice not to have to hide the weird shit happening with me. I start off in a sprint. It doesn't feel like I'm going any faster than usual, but the debris I'm kicking up indicates otherwise. I look over at Madison, and she is still holding my hand. She digs in with a short burst of speed, pulling me along with her. I watch the buildings pass us in a blur. I'm doing it. I'm really fucking doing it. I dig in to see if I have a little more to give. The moving buildings are the only indication of our actual speed. I watch as the colors blur even further. I wish I would have thought to time us. This is so freeing. We come to a sudden stop, but my feet don't get the memo. I tumble several times ... the ground not so forgiving.

"Are you okay?" Madison asks as she kneels on the ground over me.

I lie spread out on the ground, needing a moment to digest the rush. "Surprisingly, yeah! That was fucking awesome."

"You did it. Now we just have to work on your stopping." She giggles. She's actually really cute when she's not trying so hard to be a sex kitten.

"No shit," I agree. "I can't believe I was able to move

that fast. It felt like I was running fast, but not super-human like. The blur of the buildings around us was the only reason I could tell."

"You're definitely not a wolf," she informs. "You're not a warlock, and you're not a vampire. I'm more curious than ever on what you could be."

"How can you be so sure I'm not any of the things you just named?" Did I just give myself away with this little impromptu run?

"Because none of the supernaturals I named are as fast as a vampire, yet you we're able to keep up with me. You're not a vampire because your core body temp is too high."

"Was all of this a test? Just a way for you to guess what I am?" Dammit. I messed up. All it took was a pretty face and banging body for me to let my guard down. Of course she had ulterior motives.

"No. Of course not. You have to know that wasn't my intent. I was truthful when I admitted that I wanted time alone with you. You asked what my abilities were, and I saw a chance to try to impress you."

The sincerity in her eyes is coupled with what? Fear? Suddenly, I feel like an ass for making her feel defensive.

"Sorry. I'm still processing the fact I have abilities at all. Didn't mean to imply that you brought me out here just to test me. We were having a good time. And for the record, I am impressed. Thank you for showing me I can do that."

She takes a seat on the grass next to me. I didn't

expect that either. She is so put together, but she is getting her dress dirty to hang with me. A glimpse of the real her, I'm sure.

"I'm glad I could show you. I can teach you all sorts of stuff if you let me. All the rules, the work-arounds, who to watch out for, etcetera. I can be your best bud."

"I doubt the bud part," I say as I sit up. I could never look at her as one of the guys. Not with that body. "Don't you have friends that already hold that title?"

"Nah. Most of the girls are intimidated by me or shun me because their men are attracted to me. The guys mostly just want to bang me, not be my friend."

I call tell her it's the package she's presenting, but she's a smart girl. She knows how she's coming across. It's her shield, and only she can want to let that go.

"So tell me more about vampires. All I know is what I've watched on TV. Are you really dead?"

She snickers. "That's debatable. We're immortal and will never age. We're stuck at the age we get turned."

"Turned? So you weren't born a vampire?"

"No. Vampires can't reproduce. I think there are a couple of rare cases where a vampire mated with a human. One was able to carry the baby to an expedited term and the other woman died. There are rules against vampires mating with a human now, though, because of it. I was turned five years ago."

I'm so intrigued and need to know more. "How did it happen?"

"I was dating this guy at my university in Colorado.

When he first revealed that he was a vampire, I didn't believe him. We dated for almost a year, and I fell hard for him. Once he starts showing me glimpses of his abilities, I knew he wasn't lying. I begged him to turn me, and he didn't hesitate. Only I had no idea what I was truly asking for. The thirst for blood was so powerful. I hurt a few people before the council caught me. I was facing supernatural prison or attend here under probation. I chose the academy, and now my probation period is up. Now that I've adjusted to what I am, I'm just working on developing and controlling my abilities."

"That's wild. So you'll never age? You'll always look this way." I don't dwell on the fact that she just admitted that she's hurt someone before. That couldn't have been easy to share so I don't want to pry further.

"Yes. I'll always be this hot," she teases. "It's one of the perks."

"Do you have a heartbeat?"

"Yes. Unlike the TV nonsense, we do have a heartbeat. We pump blood to our organs, and that's why our skin is not cold to the touch and why we aren't pale. It's called perfusion. Let's see what other TV myths I can debunk. We eat and drink like humans. Although we don't really sleep, we do rest. The one thing that is consistent with TV is that we can't go out in sunlight unless we have a spell-infused protective piece on our person. It can be a necklace or any piece of jewelry really ... as long as we're wearing it. The academy is veiled so it blocks out the

QUANTUM ENTANGLEMENT: PART ONE

harmful UV rays. We only need the protective piece when we leave campus."

Learning about vampires has been interesting, but I've been gone for a bit. Loren and Genesis may be looking for me.

"It's been fun hanging with you a bit, but I need to get back. I'm sure Loren and Genesis are wondering where I ran off to. Thank you for educating me about vampires and the whole dashing thing."

"Okay. Sure," she says solemnly.

"Come with me. Maybe we can grab a drink and hang a bit more after the party."

I grab her hand and pull her up. She smiles and agrees to help me find the girls. Maybe I can help her make more girlfriends, and I can will my dick not to go there. She needs friends more than she needs one night in the sheets.

As soon as we arrive back at the party, we run into my roommate, Brody. "Hey, man. Two chicks were looking for you about ten minutes ago. I know Loren, but the other girl must be new."

"Did you see which way they headed?"

"No, but the one chick looked pretty messed up. She couldn't even stand straight. Loren may have taken her back to her dorm."

So the book nerd couldn't handle her liquor. I'm not surprised. She said she wasn't much of a partier to begin with. "I'm going to go check on her," I tell Madison.

"Want me to go with you?"

83

"Nah. I'll catch up with you later. Thank you again for tonight."

She doesn't look too pleased, but I have to go. I kind of feel guilty for ditching the girls I came with. Using my newfound speed, it takes me no time at all to arrive at their dorm. After a few brisk knocks, the door swings open.

"What are you doing here?" Loren asks. "It's after curfew. If Gertrude catches you, we'll all be in deep shit."

"I ran into my roommate, Brody, and he told me Genesis was drunk off her ass. I came to check on her."

Loren cross her arm across her chest and stares at me like I've grown two heads. "She's not drunk ..."

"Well, he said she looked pretty messed up and that she couldn't stand straight."

"I've got it all under control, so you can go back to hanging out with Madison."

She tries to push the door closed, but I'm too fast. I enter the room only to find Genesis doubled over on the bed. "What's wrong with her?"

"I don't know. We were walking around the party when she just crumpled to the ground like a rag doll. She screamed out in pain, but it was brief. She hasn't said much since with the exception of shaking her head when I offered to get my uncle. I brought her back here to be away from speculation."

"Something is wrong, and you don't have this under control. She may not have a choice about getting help."

I flip the lights on so I can get a better look at her.

QUANTUM ENTANGLEMENT: PART ONE

The light from the current lamps are useless. The first thing I see when I turn her to face me are the bruises on her face and arms. Her eyes glazed are over. "Get someone in here now," I boom.

"No." She's too weak to even protest.

Loren nods and then disappears. She is gone maybe ten minutes before she returns with Mr. Blakely. Fuck, why did she have to get the headmaster? I guess getting in trouble is the least of our concerns.

"She called me because I'm her uncle, and right now, I'm not worried about why you're in here afterhours. I'm here to find out what's wrong with Genesis."

The whole mind reading thing freaks me out every single time. I try not to think about it as I move aside to let him next to Genesis. He inspects her face and arms. He closes his eyes as he runs a single hand along her side and then legs. I look on in confusion.

"You did right to call me, Loren. She has three cracked ribs interfering with her breathing and a fractured left femur."

"What! How?" I exclaim.

"Impossible," Loren adds. "We were just walking when she collapsed."

"Mr. Remis, help me get her to the infirmary. Get some rest and I'll speak with you tomorrow about this party," he tells Loren. He carries Genesis out of the room so I don't know how my help comes into play, but I follow him anyway. We walk in silence until we arrive at this elaborate looking clinic.

"Is she going to be okay?" I ask finally.

"What were you doing tonight?" he asks, ignoring my question.

"What do you mean?"

"I can sense the presence of alcohol in her system. Demigods and demigoddess have the ability to heal themselves. Her human half is affected by the alcohol, thus prolonging her healing time. That's just one of the problems. The other problem is that she didn't get this injury from a simple intoxicated fall, so I'll ask again. What were you doing tonight? Or did you forget the whole connected thing?"

My throat tightens as realization dawns on me. I did this. *Fuck.* It must be from my crash landing.

"What crash landing?" he asks, reading my mind once again.

"One of the girls was showing me how to run at superhuman speed, only I didn't know how to stop. I tumbled several times, but I was okay. It didn't hurt."

"That's because Genesis absorbed all of that pain and broken bones. She felt every bit of it. So imagine running at the speed of a car going a hundred miles per hour and then crashing. Now imagine what impact that car would take. That's what your carelessness caused her tonight."

"Oh, God. I'm so sorry."

"There is a reason you're here to learn to control your powers, Mr. Remis, and this instruction doesn't come from other students. They're here to learn just like you. Now in this instance, everything you do is being felt by

Genesis. She'll heal quicker once the alcohol is gone from her system and the two halves of her can work together properly, but that doesn't mean she gets to skip the pain of doing so."

He lays her down on a stretcher, and I just want to go to her. I'm sick to my stomach with worry and regret. "What can I do? I'm so sorry," I apologize again.

"Nothing. I will ease her pain. For now, head to your room. We'll discuss this tomorrow. This is not a very good start."

I leave the infirmary, feeling like the biggest jerk. How could I have been so reckless? I totally forgot all about the whole connected thing. Knowing I've caused an injury to someone else tarnishes the fun I had with Madison. It felt so freeing in the moment, but at what cost? I'll be back first thing tomorrow. I need to know that she'll be okay. From now on, it's no longer just my safety I have to worry about. I vow to protect her from this moment forward.

CHAPTER NINE

Genesis

Light filters through the windows across from me as I look around the whitewashed room. Medical and state-of-the-art lab equipment are in abundance around the room. I grip the rails of the stretcher I'm on as I start to remember last night's events. I slowly rise while trying to untangle myself from the wires attached to me. A monitor above me begins to sound. The noise startles me, and I nearly pull out the IV inserted into my left arm. I need to get out of here and find out what's going on. Why am I here?

"Welcome back," Mr. Blakely says, ominously. "You're here because I brought you here last night."

The fact that he can read my mind doesn't even faze me much anymore. I think back to the party and vaguely remember Loren helping me back to our room. I remember the excruciating pain. "I must have blacked out," I admit.

"You'd be correct. And the alcohol you consumed had everything to do with that," he addresses, sternly. "The party you attended wasn't scheduled or approved through the appropriate channels. Add alcohol to the mix, and it warrants consequences. Who was responsible for hosting this party?"

"I don't know what's real anymore. I don't know what real anymore," I sing. I allow the lyrics of "Not Real Anymore" by Dreaming of Ghosts, Robot Koch, and Fiora to fill my mind and replace the confession of my thoughts for him to read. I won't let him get into my head and steal the truth. My eyes slide closed as I recall the harmony, the words echoing my own personal truth. I don't know what's real anymore.

"Clever," he responds. "Do you think you're the first to try this suppression of thought? I will get to the bottom of this, and those in attendance will meet with consequences. You and Mr. Remis get one pass since you haven't been here long enough to know the rules."

"I didn't drink enough to pass out," I confess. "I just wanted to knock the edge off. I'm of age and thought it'd be okay."

"I won't go into the rules right now, but I will say this." Elysian picks this time to enter what I have deduced to be the campus clinic or at the very least where they conduct their studies. "You're just in time, Mr. Remis. I was just about to discuss with Genesis the issue with last night and the cause of the escalation."

"Is she okay?" he asks, coming farther into the room.

"I can hear you, and yes, I'm fine," I respond. His eyebrows knits with worry as he gets closer to the stretcher.

"I'm so sorry, Genesis," he apologizes. His tone distraught.

"For what?" I ask confused. I look back and forth between him and Mr. Blakely, trying to decipher why the headmaster summoned him here.

"You were pretty injured last night," Mr. Blakely begins. "It was due to your connection with Elysian."

"Wait. What do you mean '*I was injured,*' and what does he have to do with it? I feel fine."

I try even harder to clear the haze of last night. All I can clearly recall is going down at the party after feeling a horrendous sharp pain.

"I'll let Mr. Remis explain his role on how you ended up here," Mr. Blakely states, turning his attention to Elysian.

"I left the party with Madison," he admits. "She wanted to show me more of the campus grounds. We were talking about her abilities, which led her to showing me how fast she can run. She made a lap around the entire academy faster than I had a chance to blink—well, maybe a few blinks. She attempted to show me how to tap into this power, and I did. Only, I wasn't able to stop, and I crashed onto the ground, flipping several times."

My eyes narrow as I will my thoughts to once again be reined in. She wanted to show him around campus, all right. She probably wanted to show him her vagina. Why did I bother covering for her to begin with? She threw the damn party and then disappeared with Elysian the first chance she got. *Conniving twat,* indeed.

"Un-hmm." Mr. Blakely clears his throat. "Just as I suspected, but Madison is not why I called Mr. Remis in here. We will deal with that next."

Crap. I let my thoughts get away from me. I don't know why that chick just rubs me the wrong way.

"Because we're connected, the injuries you sustained were because of me crashing. You absorbed my pain, like you did when Professor Winters showed us we were connected in her office yesterday morning."

"Only we now know the effect to be quite a bit more substantial. Genesis, you suffered three cracked ribs and a fractured femur. You not only absorbed his pain, but you also absorbed his actual would-be injuries," Mr. Blakely points out.

I can feel the color drain from my face. Being a nursing student, I'm all too aware of what that means, and the average healing time for fractures is a minimum of eight weeks. I feel along the intercostal space of my ribs and then inspect my left thigh. No pain.

"I kept watch over you last night," Mr. Blakely explains. "After your body rid itself of the alcohol, your human side worked in conjunction with your divinity to heal. I've already reassessed you before you awakened, and the fractures are gone."

"I can't believe it. I've never been able to heal myself before. I broke my ulna in the eleventh grade and spent eight weeks in a cast. Was I not a supernatural being back then?" I ask.

"You're a demigoddess, remember? That means that half of you was just dormant at that time. Both of you have only recently activated that part of yourselves."

"So basically, because the stud over there decided to engage in late-night power sharing, I had to suffer the consequences." It's more of a passive-aggressive statement than a question. Elysian was enjoying her company ... they were having fun. I brush the jealous ideation aside. He's allowed to be whatever to whomever. I have no claims to him just because we're connected. "Whatever. I just hope you think about how you may be hurting me next time you decide to be reckless."

"I'm so sorry," he apologizes for the third time. "It wasn't intentional. Of course I don't want to see you hurt. I will be more careful going forward."

"On to the next issue," Mr. Blakely interjects. "Stress equates to a lower temperature threshold for you. The lower temperature results in a slower metabolism, meaning a decreased ability to metabolize your alcohol intake."

"What does that all mean?" Elysian asks before I can speak.

"It means it doesn't take much alcohol to reach black-out status since I can no longer metabolize alcohol at a normal person's rate. It means now I'm officially an easy drunk."

"Pretty much," Mr. Blakely confirms. "Last night you

hit the exacta— the perfect storm."

"Exacta meaning two variables manifesting simultane-ously—like horse racing," Elysian surmise.

Mr. Blakely just nods. "I explained to Genesis that you two get a pass in this mess since you weren't briefed of the rules, but ignorance won't work the next time. There's nothing scheduled over the weekend, but I expect you both in Professor Winter's office by eight a.m. on Monday. No more indiscretions will be tolerated."

We both nod in understanding. Elysian waits for me while Mr. Blakely disconnects me from the EKG leads and takes out my IV.

"So much for us starting over, huh? Starting on a more positive note."

"It's fine," I assure. "You apologized, and it's done. There's no need to keep discussing it."

"So we're cool?"

"Sure. See you later."

I head in the opposite direction toward my dorm. What was I going to tell Loren? I don't want to lie to her, so I'm not. Nothing else would make sense anyway. What possible explanation could I give for healing broken bones overnight. I walk through the door, half expecting her to still be asleep since we were out so late. *No such luck.* She nearly tackles me with hugs the moment she sees me.

"Oh, God. Are you okay?"

"I'm fine. What are you doing up before nine?" I attempt.

"I was up most of the night with Elysian. We were

both really worried about you. He was beside himself with guilt." I have to admit I'm surprised that Elysian cared so much. Maybe I misjudged him. "What happened? Last time I saw you ... you were broken."

"The fractures are gone now," I assure.

I start from the beginning, hoping that I really can trust her. I tell her about our divinity, how I absorb Elysian's pain and injuries, how stress contributes to our uncontrolled powers, and how our hierarchy on the supernatural chain makes us a threat. She doesn't look surprised.

"Don't be mad, but Elysian shared all of this with me. I was so scared when my uncle told me you had all of those broken bones, and you looked so out of it. He came back after going with my uncle to take you to the infirmary. He told me that you would be okay once the alcohol left your system, but that didn't stop us from worrying about how you were doing until then. Later, he said that it wasn't his place to tell since the two of you hadn't decided how much you were going to share with the other students about your class."

"It's okay. I'm not mad. I get the vibe that I can trust you."

"You totally can," she promises. "I won't tell anyone."

"I just want a nice hot soak in that tub and a quiet afternoon of reading before I have to start studying on Monday. This weekend, I just want to rest and digest all of this."

"What are you studying? What is your major?"

"Psych nursing. I graduate next semester, and then I'll have board exams."

"That's pretty cool. I want to be a fashion designer," she shares. "I'm in love with everything couture."

"I have no idea what that is, but I'm fascinated by your inspiration board."

She goes to the board and plucks one of the designs off the cork. "I'm going to be famous one day, designing for all the runway models."

"I have no doubt." I smile.

"Well, enough chitchat. You've had the night from hell." She goes into the bathroom and starts to run a bath, then comes back with a wide grin. "I sprinkled some of my favorite rose-infused bath salts in it. Soak away."

"You're too much," I tease. She has been nothing but sweet since the moment we met. I'm lucky to have her for a roommate, and I can already tell we will be great friends.

"Not at all," she replies. "I'm heading out to get us some breakfast. You're going to love it. And don't worry, I won't bring you any meat. Honestly, that just means more for me."

She skips out of the room before I can protest. The heavenly scent of roses wafts from the bathroom, calling me to get into the warm, welcoming waters. I waste no time ditching the capri pants and top from last night. I undress completely before lowering myself into the silky waters. My mind wanders over to Jan and Steve. I need to call them to tell them something at least. Cooper, not so much. Yes, it stung that he broke up with me even though that's where things were headed anyway, but I think it hurt more that I wasn't a better judge of character. In the end, he wasn't someone I could count on—someone I could confess all this madness to. Having Loren to help navigate this new change in my life is a blessing. I'm connected with Elysian, but he's different. He's hot, and someone I need to keep strictly platonic. So why did it bother me so much to learn that he had spent time with Madison and shared a part of his identity with her? I have so many thoughts and unanswered questions consuming me.

This bath is great, but I can still feel an edge of stress seeping into my thoughts, making me question everything. I begin to sing "Not Real Anymore," but this time out loud. It worked once before to keep my thoughts at bay. I don't know how long I'm in the tub, but at this point, I have a whole concert of songs I've belted out. I've moved onto "Girls Just Wanna Have Fun" by Chromatics when I hear a knock and giggling on the other side of the door.

"Can we get tickets to that performance?" Loren asks.

Wait ... what? I sit up straight, sloshing water over the side of the tub. She said *we*. Oh, God. Okay, maybe it's another one of her friends that I've yet to meet.

"Who's out there?" I ask, suspiciously.

"Your other half," Elysian teases, and I want to slip underneath the water. "Don't stop now."

I'm mortified. Of course, it couldn't simply be just

another one of Loren's friends. Maybe if I stay in here long enough, he'll leave.

"Hurry up in there," Loren urges. "I've been gone for twenty minutes, and you're still in there. Your surprise breakfast is going to get cold."

I reluctantly get out of the tub. I guess hiding in here is futile. I dry off before I remember I never brought a change of clothes in here with me.

"Can you get me a pair shorts and tank out of my drawer. I forgot to bring clothes in here." I really want to say that I wasn't expecting her to come back with *him,* but I resist the urge.

I crack the door open just a tad—expecting to see her outstretched arm. Instead, it's his. I clench the towel around me tighter. His eyes peruse me with a caress before he closes the distance so I can reach the clothes.

"Loren ran to get ice down the hall for the drinks." He smirks.

"Thanks," I manage to get out before yanking the clothes out of his hand.

The towel slips ever so slightly, but he is quick to turn away. *Ugh.* He probably sees me like a little sister or some equivalent. Why do I care? Him refusing to look is obviously a testament to his lack of interest. I bet if Madison was standing here in this towel, he wouldn't be able to tear his eyes away. I quickly shut the door before I embarrass myself any further. *Too late.* Wrapped in the gym shorts, I find panties and a sports bra that he obviously picked out. At least he was smart enough to know that I couldn't possibly wear the tank without support. Still, he's touched my intimate things. I get dressed and force myself to leave the safety of the bathroom. *He's just a guy*, I chant over and over. Loren comes back in just as I enter the room. I look at all the food she has spread out and focus on that. So thoughtful.

"I got you eggs Benedict," she announces. "Without the ham. I told them to put it on my plate. Oh, and I ran into Elysian getting food so I told him to join us. Hope you don't mind."

Kind of too late if I did, but I just smile. "Of course not. Thank you for the food. You couldn't have possibly known it was one of my favorites."

"Mine too," she beams. "But I opted for the southwestern omelet this go-round. Elysian did too."

He uncovers his food, and together, they definitely have enough meat. I sit on my bed, and she passes me an orange juice.

"This is really good," I comment, honestly. "The juice too."

"Mhmm. I got the ice here. Otherwise, they fill your drink up with ice rather than actual juice. It's freshly squeezed."

"It is good," Elysian agrees with a mouth full. He decides to take a seat next to me, and I don't miss Loren's subtle eyebrow raise.

She's the one that is finding all these reasons to be around him. That has to mean she likes him, right? I'm sure we will have lots to discuss once he leaves.

CHAPTER TEN

Elysian

Genesis stretches out on her bed, her already tiny shorts rising to expose more skin. I try to forget the visual of her standing in only a towel, a flash of her pale pink nipple taunting me. I did turn away as the towel began to slip but not fast enough. My cock twitches slightly at the recall. She's off-limits. We're connected, which means we're partners in this quest to find our purpose. Any involvement that may arise with a woman would be temporary—a sexual endeavor. My hope is still with someone else, even if I give in to the urge of my physical needs. I can't blur the lines with her ... She deserves better.

"What do you have planned for today?" I ask nonchalantly. Loren has found an excuse to leave. That coupled with her enthusiasm for me join them for breakfast are a good indication that she's trying to play matchmaker.

"Read. Nap. Maybe read some more," Genesis ponders.

"That sounds boring," I tease. "We're about to be inundated with a hectic course load as well as our studies from our main universities. Is that the only thing you can think of, knowing this may be the last of our free time?"

I have since moved to sit on Loren's bed. Our proximity wasn't doing my hardening cock any favors. It couldn't care less about our connection or what she deserves. She sits up to pull her ginger red locks into a ponytail, a move so simple yet so sexy.

"What do you propose I do then?" she asks, arching a single brow at me.

"Spend the day with me," I suggest. "I found a creek along the edge of the campus that's still inside the allowed perimeter. We can take a picnic, soak up some rays, go for a swim, and just spend the day getting to know each other. We may even discover how we're connected."

"You mean we can see if we have any commonalities that may link us ... like family, etcetera."

"Exactly."

If I'm being honest, I find myself wanting to spend time with her, but exploring our history can be beneficial too.

"I guess it couldn't hurt. I can always read and nap tomorrow," she admits. "Let me just change into my swimsuit underneath this. Do you need to go back to your room and change too?"

"Yeah. I have a few things I need to do first, so I'll

meet you back here in an hour. Give me your number and I'll text you once I'm outside."

She calls out each digit, and I enter them into my phone. I snap a quick pic to add to her contact, but she catches me.

"Ugh. Why would you take a pic now when I look like crap?"

She adjusts her ponytail, and I snap another pic. Now I'm just fucking with her. She could never look like crap. She's freaking gorgeous. Her glacial clear eyes pin me to the spot.

"I took a second one just in case," I joke. She answers by turning her phone toward me to take a pic. I wink, and she rolls her eyes. "I better get going to get changed." I wink again.

Normally, my winks melt panties, so I find it hilariously interesting that it annoys the hell out of her. Maintaining a platonic relationship is going to take the will of a god, and I'm only half.

I pull up outside Genesis's building on my motorcycle and text her to come out. She appears before I even hit send, her jaw slack with awe. I school my features as she comes down the sidewalk in the sexiest *fuck me* denim shorts that I've ever seen. The roundness of her ass hugs the fabric like a second skin. This girl is stacked, and my dick greatly appreciates the curves. *She's off-limits. She's off-limits.*

I repeat this mantra as she gets closer, thankful that my shades hide what my eyes may give away. *Lust.*

"Am I supposed to get on that?" She looks at it incredulously.

"Don't worry, sweetheart. You're in expert hands." I pass her a helmet and a backpack before leaning the bike slightly to the side for her to get on.

"Mhmm. I hope being a supernatural also means we have extra lives. Still, try not to kill us."

She dons the helmet and backpack before sliding in behind me. Her petite frame snuggles against mine as she secures her arms around my waist. My dick stirs yet again. A fresh ocean scent with hints of floral permeates the air around me.

"I got us, baby. Don't you worry."

I feel her stiffen behind me at the endearment. I don't know why I just called her baby since it's normally a term I reserve for my ex. I have to admit her reaction pleases me, though. Maybe I get under skin just like she gets under mine. Maybe it wouldn't hurt to explore that too. *Harmless flirtation.*

"Are you fucking with me?" she asks after a beat of silence.

"I don't know. Would you like me to ... fuck with you, I mean?" Now that's how you serve up an innuendo. *Hard, fast, and unexpected.* I rev the engine to drown out the snark that I'm sure is to follow and pull away with a grin of accomplishment. She makes my cock desperate with need, so why shouldn't I have a little fun?

"No thank you, stud. Save it for Madison. I'm sure she'd love to introduce you to her vagina," she admonishes over the hum of the engine.

"Careful, love. Your jealousy is showing."

"You wish."

The rest of the short ride is quiet. I know I've struck a nerve. Can I be right? Was she jealous of me hanging out with Madison? I definitely plan on finding out.

When we arrive at the creek, I cut the engine and lean the bike once again so she can get off first. "The water looks so inviting," she notes, already walking toward the creek.

By the time I park the bike, she's already removing her shorts and tank. Holy fuck me. Her heart-shaped ass warrants a touch, but I can't. Her body is even more tempting than I could have imagined or yet tried not to imagine. She wastes no time getting into the water. I use this time to remove the blanket and lunch I packed within the backpack. Once I have everything laid out, I decide to join her. I remove my clothes down to my board shorts and jump in.

"So aren't you glad you got out of that stuffy room?" I tease, treading water in front of her.

"I can admit I needed this. Even though I think you like fucking with me. I fuck back, you know."

"Do you now?" I chuckle at her audacity of a late comeback. She is in the minor leagues against my ability to deliver an innuendo. Nice try, though. "Reverse cowgirl, I hope." I add a wink for good measure.

"You're insufferable," she accuses. "Did you invite me out just to play with me?" She splashes me in the face with water and tries to run. *In water* of all things.

I grab her and pull her to me in one swift move. Her hand presses against my rock-hard abs ... a few inches south, and she'd find that my stomach isn't the only thing hard. She breathes out in a pant as my hands inch down her waist.

"What was that? You fuck back? I fuck harder." I pull her closer until her stomach is against my cock—to show her how much I'm playing.

"Okay, you win," she recuses, pushing away from me. My hard-on is unmistakable. I watch as all the color drain from her gorgeous face. I definitely get under her skin. I make her nervous. I make her want things she knows she shouldn't. But above all else, I bet I make her sweet pussy wet.

I follow her out of the water. She picks up one of the towels I pulled from the backpack and begins to dry off. I pick up the other one and dry myself too. She's still flushed.

"Oh, my goodness. How did you find this spot? Not many know it's here." Madison laughs, appearing from nowhere. "I hope I'm not intruding. This is my favorite place to relax on the weekend."

"Oh, not at all," Genesis speaks up, giving me a look that it's definitely an intrusion.

"I see you two have a picnic set up. Are you sure?"

"Join us. We're just taking some time to unwind

before our hectic schedule starts on Monday," I encourage. If Genesis wants to act like her arrival is welcome, then who am I to say different?

Madison takes a seat on the blanket closest to me and begins to look through the food containers. "That's a good idea. Balancing your studies here with your other university classes is going be rough."

"Don't I know it."

Genesis has yet to utter another word. She finds a spot on the blanket and schools her features to look unbothered.

"So, in fun news, I got busted by the headmaster for throwing that party without permission. Having alcohol involved just added fuel to the fire," Madison informs.

"How did he find out?"

"I don't know." She looks over at Genesis. "It's hard to believe that one of the attendees would rat me out. My punishment affects them too."

"What do you mean?"

"There is a ban on all parties for the next few weeks," she continues. "So nobody is allowed to throw a party. That and I have to do community service type work for the headmaster next week," she huffs.

"I'm so sorry," I reply, genuinely.

"Meh. It is what it is. Did you get this food from Canyon's?" she asks, changing the subject.

"Yes. I got it for Genesis. She's a vegetarian." This piques her interest. "It's their yellow curry bowl."

"What's in it?" she asks as she take the container from me.

"Yellow curry chickpeas, potatoes, carrots, and red cabbage."

"It smells heavenly," she admits, taking her first bite. "And it's absolutely delicious. Thank you for this," Genesis says.

"This is all really sweet of you, Elysian. You're a good friend," Madison adds.

I don't miss her emphasis on the word *friend*. Neither does Genesis if that wrinkle in her brow is any indication.

"We're the two newbies. We have zero knowledge on how all of this work amongst you that have transitioned into your advanced studies. She and I have to stick together and support each other through this journey."

"You don't have to feel like it's just you two against the world. We all had to start somewhere, but our abilities are only a small piece of who we are. Besides ... you have me. I told you that I'll help you navigate through this."

"And I appreciate that," I assure.

"I like these little containers," she mentions, changing the subject again.

"Yeah. My stuff finally arrived. I packed the food I bought from Canyon's in them to prevent spillage on the ride here."

"I noticed your bike when I came up. Sweet ride," she compliments.

"Thank you. I'm glad she finally made it here."

"Your bike is a she?"

I nod. "Shelby is my ride or die. She's named after my ex."

"You must really love her," Genesis says. For Madison's benefit, I'm sure.

"Yeah. She's my first love. Not sure if things are final, but it's not up to me."

"You should go out with us tonight," Madison says suddenly. Changing the subject once again. I'm learning that's her go-to when she gets uncomfortable with a topic.

"Who is us, and I thought there was a ban on parties?" I question as I finally eat some of the food.

"There is a ban," she reiterates. "I never said the party was on campus."

"Oh, Genesis and I haven't earned off-campus privileges yet. The headmaster mentioned it, but I don't know how it all works other than we wouldn't be able to find our way back here without permission."

She laughs. "Of course they're going to tell the newbies that. We know better. We know all the loopholes that they've yet to discover."

"Okay. Let's hear it." I ignore the obvious disapproval etched in Genesis's face. She has a poor poker face.

"How do I know that the two of you won't snitch? If I share, then you have to come so that you're both just as accountable."

"Elysian, you remember what Mr. Blakey said. We only get that one pass," Genesis warn.

"If the party police don't agree, then I'm not sharing

our intel. She's probably the one who got me busted," Madison accuses, her eyes narrowing at Genesis.

"What if we accidentally use our powers and it sends off another beacon? What if we hurt someone? There's a reason they insist we stay here and not leave the campus until we can control our abilities," Genesis argues.

"Ummm. I said there was a loophole." Madison all but rolls her eyes.

"You guys do what you want. I'll leave, so I don't have to hear your big secret. You don't have to worry about me saying a word."

Genesis gets up and snatches her clothes off the blanket. She storms off in a huff but doesn't get far with my super speed. "Don't leave. Let's hear what she has to say. If there is a way for us to leave campus safely, I'd love to get in contact with my buddy and my parents. I know you'd love to get in touch with your family and friends too."

I see her wavering. "I don't have a good feeling about this but seeing my family would be nice. I just don't trust her."

"You don't have to. Trust me. We're connected, meaning I will always look out for you."

"*Ugh*. Fine, but if we get kicked out, we're in this together. And I'm telling you now ... I'm not keeping this from Loren."

"Oh, you won't have to. Loren is going. She's the main one who helped discover the loophole." She laughs.

"Whatever. What's the big loophole? I'm in," Genesis

acquiesces.

"In our Elite circle, we have friends that are witches. Advanced witches. You give them a piece of inconspicuous jewelry, and they create a reverse locator spell with it. While worn, you will be able to find your way back here to the academy. It also binds your power to the jewelry so you don't accidentally use your powers while worn. Now here is the hard part—"

"That wasn't the hard part?" I interrupt.

"It was. But here is where things get tricky," Madison explains. "We need either Professor Winters, Professor Guenther, or Mr. Blakely to let down the veil. Without this step, we can't see the perimeter we need to cross to reach the outside of the academy. We can't simply mass exodus out the front gate."

"But why would they let down the veil, and where do we exit?" Genesis asks.

"A gate actually surrounds the whole campus. We're currently in the back of the academy. There is one other exit besides out the front gate, and that's across the creek from where we are now."

"I don't see a gate," Genesis challenges.

"That's because it's veiled from within the perimeter. The gates that you can actually see with the exception of the front gate are an illusion. The actual barrier is far beyond that. Now the *why* part. Ancillary staff don't all reside here. You have to be a supernatural being to work here, but for many, this is a job to sustain their livelihood. They have a family that they go home to. The two professors named and the headmaster are the only three that can grant exit and entrance. They don't all stay here either. They rotate so that at least one of them remains on campus at all times. Whoever remains behind, grants the in and out for these workers. To do that, they must let the veil down at scheduled times because the workers aren't allowed to have unlimited access to the academy."

"Ah, so like the cooks, housekeeping, and other faculty members?" I question.

"To name a few. There are groundskeepers, restaurant owners, and so many other people that I can't name all the jobs. The point is, we must leave and return on a set schedule. *No exceptions*. We must be out of our dorms no later than nine thirty p.m. before the resident monitor does rounds at ten p.m. They won't check the individual rooms. They just make sure the opposite sex isn't seen or heard inside a dorm room during their walk-through. They make rounds every thirty minutes starting at ten. We have to meet here before ten p.m. At that time, the veil comes down for exactly five minutes to allow the workers to exit. This is when we are actually able to see the gate in order to leave."

"So every worker here gets off at ten p.m.?" That's kind of weird.

"Of course not, but since most staff are on a rotating schedule, we're not privy to every single time the veil is let down. Ten p.m. is the last time, though— the time that all workers must exit if they plan to leave the campus for the night. Since that is the one constant, we use that as our go time. The other constant is five a.m. It's the first time the veil is let down for the workers to come back to work."

"So we all leave at ten p.m., but we have to stay out until five a.m. when the unveiling happens?"

"You got it. Only six of us are privy to this info and making the trip. With you two, it makes eight."

"Yeah, the more people that know, the greater chance that the secret gets out. You don't have to worry about us saying anything."

"What he said," Genesis adds.

"Okay. Great. So to make sure you two can make the outing tonight, I need you to bring me a piece of jewelry. Nothing flashy or that will draw attention. Melissa and Haley will cast the reverse locator spell and bind your powers to the jewelry."

"Do you guys do this every weekend?" Genesis asks.

"Usually on Saturdays when less staff are here to begin with, but it's definitely a planned outing. We decide as a group at the beginning of each week. At least half of our small group must agree, or we abort for that weekend. No solo trips. You will be on the outside without your powers since it's also bound by the jewelry with the reverse locator spell and this academy. We leave as a group and return as group. If you decide to do something on your own once we're on the outside, that's fine. We just need a way to stay in contact in case we run into trouble."

"That sounds fair," Genesis responds, surprising us both.

"Awesome. Bring the jewelry you want to use for the spell by six p.m. tonight. Elysian, I'll give you my number."

I don't even look over at Genesis as I exchange numbers with Madison. Jealousy is a vibe, and I can feel that shit radiating off my back.

"The food was amazing. Thank you for letting me crash your get-together. I'll see you both later."

Genesis waits until Madison is out of sight to comment. "I still don't trust her, but I'm trusting you. Oddly, I believe you have my back. So I'm going to go out on a limb here and not be the rule follower. If this works, I can go see my adoptive parents. I won't tell them what I am, but maybe I can get them to shed some light on who my biological parents are."

"Yeah, I can arrange for my buddy Josh to visit and call my folks. A little normalcy to hold on to will make this whole transition more tolerable." I begin to pack up the uneaten food, containers, blanket, and towels. "Sorry we were interrupted, but at least some good came out of it. Let's reschedule this get to know each other session for tomorrow. We can have a Nick at Nite marathon."

"Sounds cool as long as you check your crassness at the door," she warns.

"I'll try."

We get back on Shelby and head back toward the dorms. Tonight is going to be an adventure, but I'm ready to take back some of my autonomy. Six can't come fast enough.

CHAPTER ELEVEN

Genesis

I can't believe it. We're on the outside of the academy. We follow Madison through the woods in pairs. Elysian grabbed my hand so we weren't separated, and he still hasn't let go. Our steps are in sync as we walk hand in hand. I clutch the pendant around my neck, hoping the casted spell bound to it works. Each step takes us farther away from safety.

"We've made it," Madison announces as we're the last to arrive at the clearing. We're now standing in a small parking lot of an abandoned building. "Our ride is only a few minutes away."

She looks down at our joined hands. Elysian must notice this too. He slowly untangles his fingers from mine. I immediately miss the warmth of his fingers.

"Where are we headed?" I ask.

"Club Fusion and then food after it closes at two a.m. We will arrive back here at four twenty a.m. to allow time for the hike back to the academy before the veil comes down at five a.m."

I want to ask more questions, but a SUV pulls up. The others waste no time getting in, so I follow their lead. I guess we're sticking together, so I'll treat this as a trial run. If things go smoothly, then next time, I'll opt for some time to see Jan and Steve.

"I've got something for you," Loren says as she scoots in next to me. I haven't seen much of her today, but she did confirm that these little rendezvous originated from her plan.

"What is this?" I ask as she passes me her tote.

"A change of clothes. I didn't get a chance to tell you to dress for the club and to wear sneakers for the short hike. Once we get to the parking lot, we change into our heels."

I look around the three rows of seating, and she's right. Everyone is dressed for the club, even Elysian, who is currently sitting in the middle row talking to the only other two guys that are going with us. The romper I'm wearing is cute and goes great with my sandals, but it's a far cry from club wear. I pull out a black spandex dress. Looks simple enough. Strappy black heels sit at the bottom of the tote.

"This is cute. Thank you." I smile. "I don't know how much good advanced notice would have done anyway. I don't own anything like this."

"You're welcome. Now let's get you changed."

"What? Where? You mean right now?" Surely, that's not what she means.

"I'll cover you. Just pull your romper down to your waist and then slip the dress over your head. Easy peasy. Nobody is going to look back here."

"We won't look," Elysian mocks as he turns to stare at me. "Just be quick so we aren't tempted."

"Come on. Don't antagonize her," Loren pleads. "We're heading straight to the club, and we need her to change now, so eyes forward."

He winks at me before turning back around. Loren shields me with her body, but it doesn't do much good if somebody chooses to look back here. Not to mention the passing cars. Can they see inside the SUV? I need to stop overthinking it. I quickly pull the romper down to my waist and slip the unforgiving fabric over my head. Without warning, Loren unsnaps my bra and gives it a pull. I work quickly to get the dress over my now exposed breasts.

"What was that?" I whisper hiss.

"That bra won't go with the dress. Well, no bra would. You'll see."

I'm already questioning if I should have been so quick to accept the change of clothes. I lift my butt from the seat so I can push the romper down my legs and pull the dress down. The length leaves much to be desired, so I'll have to pull it down some once we're out of the SUV. I put my romper in the tote and change into the heels. We pull into club valet, and my nerves begin to kick in. This place is huge.

I'm the last to get out with Loren's help. I tug at the hemline of the form-fitting dress, but it's evident that I'm lucky to even have my ass covered because it's not going past my mid-thigh. The swell of my breasts peeps through the keyhole of the dress, and the back of the dress is completely open.

"That's some dress," Elysian comments as he peruses me, walking a circle around me to survey every detail.

"Hush it. You don't have to tell me how ridiculous I look. I feel like a streetwalker. That's it. I'm changing back into my romper."

"Oh, to the contrary. You look smoking hot. Let's just fix your hair."

"What's wrong with it?" I frown. He grabs the pins from the bun I spent thirty minutes perfecting and watches as my hair tumbles wildly past my breasts. He gives it a few fluffs, and I finally push his hands away.

"After you." He smirks.

I walk past, feeling his eyes on my ass. We bypass the line forming around the building without having to show any ID. One of the brunette witches—Kristin, I believe her they said her name was—has some serious connections with this place.

"He likes you," Loren teases.

"And that's why he's already sped up to catch up with Madison," I challenge. "He's a big flirt. His innuendos are nothing short of personal entertainment until he gets his girl back."

"I don't know. We'll see, but tonight, he's not your only prospect. Wait until you see all the heads you turn in that dress."

She grabs my wrist and steers me toward a bar to our left. The rest our group disappears through the crowd. Rock music pumps at decibels loud enough to make you go deaf. Loren's lips are moving but trying to actually hear her is a struggle. Once we get farther away from the dance floor, her words become audible. I ignore her turning heads remark.

"We'll meet the group upstairs in VIP in a moment. I just wanted a chance to get you alone and see what's up with you and Elysian. Like I said, I think he likes you, and I know he took you on a picnic. Madison said she ran into you two at the creek." She turns and order two Long Islands and two shots of tequila before returning her attention back to me.

"The picnic was supposed to be just us getting to know each other and comparing our history to see if we can figure out how we're entangled. If you like him, then by all means, go for it. I don't think he's emotionally available, but if that's what you're interested in, then go for it."

"Can you stop saying go for it? I'm not interested in him for me. I was trying to get you on that before Madison gets her way with him." She passes me one of the Long Islands and a shot of tequila. "Drink up. Time to let loose," she says, clicking her shot glass with mine.

I knock back the tequila and chase it with the Long Island. *Disgusting.* My eyebrows lift at how strong the drink is. I have to be mindful of what happened the last time I drank alcohol.

"She can have him," I insist. "What's up with the two of you, anyway? You call Madison a conniving twat, but then you participate in these escape excursions with her."

"We have mutual friends. Basically, the group here with us tonight. We're the Elite Eight, but I'll tell you about our little group later. One of the guys isn't here with us tonight. I tolerate Madison, but that doesn't mean I'm not aware of how fake she is. She will use people to get what she wants, and she thinks that she's God's gift, and everyone should be grateful for her presence. Trevor and I used to date until she slept with him."

Trevor is one of the guys that came along with us. Tall and slender with a swimmer's build. Now her disdain for Madison makes sense. It's always a guy. "Did she know that the two of you were dating?"

"She said she didn't, but he and I went everywhere together. We weren't official, but we were dating. She knew I liked him."

"And what was Trevor's excuse?" I take a few more sips of my Long Island, the buzz already filtering through my veins.

"Of course, he said it was a mistake—a one-time thing. At the moment, he rationalized that I wasn't his girlfriend, so we were both free to see other people. It hurt, but I got over it. I forgave them both, but I won't forget."

"You're too hot to get hung up on someone who tries to justify sleeping around. I'm not looking for a man, but I'll be your wing woman." I grin.

"Let's go meet up with group." She laughs.

I get upstairs just in time to see Madison gyrating against Elysian on the smaller dance floor. R&B vibes up here contrast with the rock playing downstairs. Kristin passes us a glass of champagne from the bottle chilling at the table reserved for us. Loren gives me a knowing look as she takes in the performance between the stud and the twat. She couldn't possibly rub her ass any harder against his cock. I can feel my lips purse as my grip tightens around my champagne flute.

"Smile, beautiful," a preppy blonde says. His eyes twinkle with interest. "Come dance with me."

Normally, someone telling me to smile is annoying in and of itself, but I do. I smile big. He presents me with an opportunity to show Elysian that he's not the only one that can flirt. Rhianna's "Loveeeeeee Song" begins to play as I let this handsome stranger lead me to the dance floor. He immediately backs me into his chest and hardness before beginning to sway with me. His hands caress my shoulders as I let my head fall back against his chest. It's not long before he brazenly skims his hands down to my hips.

"You don't know all the wicked things I'd like to do to your body," he whispers against the shell of my ear.

"Beat it, buddy. You're barking up the wrong tree," Elysian warns out of nowhere.

"Screw you," I slightly slur. "Why don't you go back to your public dry humping with Madison?"

"No can do, sweetheart. I told you that I'll always have your back, and right now, you're intoxicated. If you were sober, you could screw this guy's brains out, and I wouldn't intervene." He gives the guy a death glare—a silent warning.

"I'm perfectly fine, so you're free to go." The guy backs away with his hands up. I didn't even get his name. "That was totally uncalled for."

"That was for your benefit. You'll thank me tomorrow," he promises.

"Bullshit! You're such a cockblocker," I slur again.

"Hate to break it to you, love, but you don't have a cock. And that slur of yours just proves my point about you being intoxicated."

"*Ugh*," I groan. I push past him and head straight to grab another flute of champagne from our table. I down the contents before Elysian can snatch the bubbly goodness away. "Too late," I sing. I stick my tongue out for added emphasis.

"Real mature," he deadpans. "But congrats. You've earned yourself a designated babysitter for the night."

"Seriously. I'm fine. Don't let me ruin your and Madison's time being humping buddies."

"Careful, sweets. Your jealousy is showing again."

"Who's jealous?" Madison interrupts.

"Oh, I was teasing Genesis because she is already drunk. She's jealous that I can hold my liquor better than she can," he covers.

Madison believes his lie. "Well, let her rest for a bit. I want to show you something." She passes me a bottled water.

"Ummmm. I'm supposed to be looking out for Genesis."

I can hear the hesitation in his voice, and that stings. He feels obligated to make sure I'm okay, but he wants to leave with Madison. I'm sure the something is her vagina, and I'm sure he knows this, hence the hesitation.

"Just go already. I'm not going to fuck this up for everybody. I'm going sit here and sip on this water."

Elysian looks at me one more time, unsure, but leaves with Madison. I meant what I said. I have no plans of being the one everyone has to worry about. I'm too occupied with suspicion of why it bothered me to see that he wanted to leave with her or if he would fuck her? I've avoided his type and for good reason. Guys like him go for the Madisons, so what the hell am I doing? Well, besides trying to convince myself I don't like him in that way. I sit back farther and watch the people dance, drink, and everything that I'm not. This was a mistake. Next time, I'm opting to see Jan and Steve. I just need a good explanation on why it is I'm seeing them so late. I'd rather see them and a few friends from the university than have a front row seat to Madison and Elysian's hookup chronicles.

At some point, I become the table watcher for all of our things while they all go out to mingle. Elysian has been by a few times to check on me, but this time, he takes a seat next to me.

"You shouldn't be sitting here alone. That's okay, though. I'm here now. How are you feeling?"

"Like I want to be alone," I reply, sarcastically. "I've managed fine all night without you, so I promise you I'm good."

"You told me to go," he argues. "You can't be pissed that I actually went."

Oh, I can, but that doesn't mean I'm going let him think I'm jealous. "I'm not pissed that you left with her. Just stop coddling me."

"You got it."

He doesn't say a word to me for the rest of the night. Instead, I watch him get drinks for Madison and tear up the dance floor with her. Loren checked on me a few times, and I assured her that I was okay. I gave it the old college try, but this is just not my scene. Watching the man that I refuse to admit I have a crush on have a good time with another woman isn't my scene either. When the DJ announces last call for alcohol, my ears perk up. It's almost closing time, and I'm ready to get out of here. My enthusiasm takes a nosedive when I remember the second half of our plans—to find an all-night spot and get some food. The veil doesn't come down until five a.m.

Fifteen minutes later, we're waiting for valet to pull the SUV around. Elysian still isn't speaking to me. He won't even look at me. I know I was a bitch to him when he was just trying to look out for me, and it's not his fault that his big brother act was pissing me off. He surely didn't treat Madison that way. Once we get into our ride, I climb to the back and kick off the heels. Feeling more sober, I decide that I'm not getting out at our next stop. The ride to the diner was short, but it gave me enough time to solidify my decision.

"Aren't you getting out?" Loren asks after I'm the only left in the SUV. The group is already heading inside. "I got a bit of a headache, and the bright light inside the diner doesn't look ideal," I say, knowing that's only a part of it. I've had my fill of watching the Elysian and Madison show. I think Loren knows too.

"If you change your mind, come and find us, okay?"

I nod, but I won't change my mind. She closes the door and heads inside the diner. I lay out on the seat and close my eyes. Sleep overcomes me, and I don't resist.

CHAPTER TWELVE

Elysian

I lie in my bed, thinking about last night as I bounce a tennis ball against my headboard. Genesis really got under my skin with her bouts of jealousy even though I admit that some of my acts were purposely to give her what she was asking for. She pushed me on Madison and then got pissed that I followed through with her repeated suggestion. Nothing happened last night. Madison showed me the rooftop of the club and gave me a tour of the entire club, introducing me to people who have no idea she's a vampire. She genuinely enjoyed my company, which was a nice change. I think she understands that friendship is all that I'm offering at the moment.

I get up and shower. It's already one in the afternoon. I didn't even lie down until six a.m. I have no idea what I'm going to do with the rest of the day. Yesterday, I told Genesis that she and I could make up for our interrupted picnic today, but after last night, I don't think it's a good idea.

After getting dressed, I call my buddy, Josh. I listen intently as he tells me how preparation for wrestling season is going. He explains that he understands that I had to go back home due to family matters and that the team wasn't upset with me. Yeah, family matters as in one of my biological parents is a god, and the parents I grew up thinking were my folks may not be at all. At least now I know the lie that was told on my behalf to get my classes transferred to online. I ask about Shelby, and he reluctantly tells me that she is seeing someone from the debate team. I don't let on how much this crushes my spirit, but what am I hanging on for? She's clearly not, so I need to let go for us both.

I end the call and open my door with the intent to just explore more of the campus. Madison pauses with her fist midair, her knock suspended. "Oh, hey." She smiles. "Looks like I almost missed you."

"Yeah. Nothing official. Just thought I'd explore more of the campus."

She looks super casual in her short cutoffs and tank, hair in a French braid. I actually think she looks better this way. Understated sexiness without trying too hard.

"Well, I stopped by just in time. Sundays are for reflection. Plus, I want to finally officially introduce you to our Elite Eight. You briefly met everyone last night except James. We like to gather near the creek to show what we've learned in the past week. It's like show and tell, but with our powers."

"Unfortunately, I wouldn't be able to participate. Other than the running thing you showed me, I've yet to tap into anything else."

"Nobody is going to expect you to give us a demonstration. Your first class isn't until tomorrow. Just come and watch. It's both informative and entertaining."

I don't want to pass on a chance to see my peers in action or to find out what this whole Elite Eight is about. "Count me in," I agree.

"Sweet. I was headed there now after I checked to see if you wanted to come."

"I know it's a bit of a trek, so let's take my bike."

Her eyes light up with excitement. "I wondered if I'd ever get to ride with you. Your bike is so edgy and bad boy like. The jury is still out on you, though. Your tattoo sleeves are quite the contradiction. You don't come off as the typical bad boy, but something tells me you just haven't shown that side of you yet."

"I definitely walk to the beat of my own drum, so I guess you'll just have to see for yourself."

She wastes no time climbing on the back of Shelby. Her arms wrap around my waist, under my Henley T-shirt. She toys with the muscles she finds there, not letting a moment to flirt pass. The ride is short, but as we come to a rolling stop, I see a small group has already gathered. *Including Loren and Genesis.* Her eyes meet mine before she looks downward. Unfounded guilt gnaws at me, but why? She's the one who decided how we were going to act with each other.

I lean my bike to the side so that Madison can get off. She winks at me before joining the group.

"Nice bike, man," one of the lanky guys compliments. "I'm Matt from last night."

"Thanks, man. I remember."

"I'm James," a taller redheaded guy introduces. His red hair is a few shades darker than Genesis. He towers over my five-feet-ten frame with much broader shoulders. "Sorry, I couldn't make it last night. I heard that it was a blast."

"Nice to meet you, man. It was a blast for sure."

I take a seat on the ground next to Madison, which happens to be directly across from Genesis. She picks at the grass next to her, anything not to return my gaze. Our group forms a circle around a fire pit, so let's see how long she can pretend she doesn't see me.

"Break out the booze." Madison chuckles. "Don't tell me you all were waiting until I got here." The nods around the circle confirm that is exactly the case. It's becoming more evident just how much clout she has here at this academy, and maybe that's my appeal. I couldn't care less about popularity and status. If you're cool to be around, then that's enough for me. "Well, we have two newbies in our midst—Elysian and Genesis. Let's give them a warm welcome by introducing ourselves and our class."

I've scanned our circle for a quick count, and there are

ten of us—six girls and four guys, including myself. I listen intently as they introduce themselves and whether they're a witch, warlock, werewolf, or vampire.

"My name is Genesis, and I'm a demigoddess," she blurts. When the fuck did we decide to tell everybody what we are? I know—*we didn't*. No discussion at all.

The circle goes completely quiet, including Madison. "Holy shit. What about you, Elysian. Are you a demigod?" she asks.

Well, the secret is out of the fucking bag, so what else can I say? "Yeah," I murmur.

"Dude! Do you even know what that means?" lanky guy Matt questions with excitement.

I pinch the bridge of my nose. Let the flood gates of fuckery begin. "We've been given the CliffsNotes version of the class." I sigh.

"It means you're going to be two of the most badass motherfuckers once you have your shit under control. I don't even think we have half gods here on Earth. We've learned a little history of gods and half gods in our curriculum, but it was enough to know that you're at the top of the pyramid when it comes to abilities—right underneath gods," he continues.

"Pyramid of abilities?" I inquire.

"Basically, the only supernatural with greater ability than a demigod or demigoddess is a god. That makes you a threat."

There goes that word again— *threat*. Thanks, Genesis.

"Look. We're just here to learn. Neither Genesis nor I asked for this. We're not a threat."

"Sorry to break it to you, babe, but that's not something you can disown and it be so. But we're not judging. We really invited you out here to invite you to join our Elite squad so we'd have your back," Madison assures. The group collectively agrees with a nod.

"What exactly is the Elite Eight?" I ask.

"As I mentioned at that first party, most classes stick with their coven, clan, or pack. Our group is a mix of all the classes. Yes, we interact with our own class, but we choose to branch out. Our circle is the most coveted group on campus. We're the best looking, best dressed, and most popular."

"No offense, but it sounds kind of pretentious," Genesis points out. "I'm not a mean girl."

"None of us are," Madison corrects. "We don't treat people poorly. We just choose to keep our circle small and do our own thing. We're not antisocial. We throw parties and invite others, but I guess the closest thing you can compare us to is a fraternity or sorority. Besides, it's not like we're snobs. That's the Legends."

"Legends?" Genesis prod.

"Legends Supernatural Academy is the other academy. They have two campuses—one here in Washington State and another one in Washington DC," Madison explains. "The faculty wouldn't have mentioned either of them. It's for the true elite. The family of politicians, celebrities, etcetera. Basically, being famous is the entry criteria."

"I'll pass. That academy doesn't sound like my cup of tea. I'm more of a down to earth kind of guy. Anyway, why invite us into your Elite? What do we have to do?" I ask.

"Nothing. We vibed from the beginning. And now finding out that the two of you are half gods adds to our diversity. You don't have a coven, clan, or pack, but you have an Elite—an inclusion of them all."

"Well, thank you for welcoming us into your Elite Eight. That's kind of rad to have such a diverse group. A community within a community per se. Like my wrestling team. I had friends outside the team, but those guys were like my family. I trusted them like no other."

"Exactly," Matt agrees. "Now you get it."

"Now that's settled, let's get this show and tell going," Matt suggests. "Melissa, Haley, Loren, and Kristin are witches. James and Trevor are werewolves. That leaves Madison and me. We're vampires and move fast."

I blink as he lifts me and takes me to the other side of the fire pit next. Now I'm standing next to Genesis. My jaw slacks.

"He's even faster than I am," Madison warns. I know how fast she is, and I can't imagine anyone going faster than that.

I'm in awe as I watch each person introduce their powers. Witches mostly rely on spells and their Grimoire, which nobody knows its location. The werewolves show off their speed and strength, while the vampires compete to see who's faster.

"I've learned how to do something else," Madison

shares vividly. She walks directly over to me and pulls my face down to hers, staring me down. "I think you have the hots for Genesis. If you do, then go kiss her."

"What? Why would I do that? I don't want to kiss her."

"How did that not work?"

"Somebody wasn't paying attention in class that day," Matt teases. "Gods and half gods can't be compelled."

"Compel what? Why would you tell me to kiss her?" I huff.

"Don't be upset. It was just a small test. Vampires can compel people to do as they say without question. Obviously, it works on humans, but I just wanted to see if it worked on supernaturals too."

"Not cool," I chastise.

"Well, I like to think that I've uncovered another one of your abilities. You can resist compulsion."

I walk back to where I originally was and take a seat. Several hours pass and night begins to fall. James lights the fire pit as more beer is handed out. I watch as he takes a seat next to Genesis. I haven't spoken to her since last night at the club. The last thing I want is to start our classes tomorrow with this awkwardness between us.

"Hey, Genesis. Can I talk with you for a minute?" She looks over the flames at me, unsure. "Just for a bit."

She says something to James, who just sat next to her, before rising to her feet.

"What do you want?" she asks once we're some distance away from the group.

"Look, I don't know why things are so weird between us, but I just wanted a chance to talk."

"Oh, you mean like we were supposed to do today before you blew me off and then rolled up here with Madison on your bike."

"Do you like me, Genesis?"

Her face contorts before she blows an exasperated breath. "Don't be so narcissistic."

She walks ahead to the edge of the creek. She picks up a few stones and skips them across the water.

"Okay. What is it then? You're constantly pushing me on Madison, but then appear jealous when I talk to or show up with her."

I pick up a few stones of my own, skipping them farther than her attempt.

"I don't have to push her on you. She does that all on her own. I'm not jealous. I purposely stay away from people like you. Like her."

"Like me? What about me?" She kneels to collect more stones.

"Never mind. Forget that I even said anything."

"No can do, sweetheart. You can't make a judgmental statement like that and then tell someone to forget it. So what about me? Because I can promise whatever you're thinking, you're wrong."

"Okay," she begins, using the end of her shirt to hold her collection of rocks. "You're the pretty boy ... the jock all the girls chase. You're the cool guy all the guys want to be like. You're the reason we got invited into this Elite.

135

You're used to using your winks, smirks, and shameless innuendos to get whatever you want. You make a girl feel special and then turn it off when you move on to your next plaything."

"Is that it? I made you feel special, and now you think I'm moving on to Madison?"

"Don't be a jerk! Of course not. Is that the only thing you took away from everything I said?"

"You mean everything you accused me of. I'm none of the things you said. Do I think I'm attractive? Of course. That's just having a healthy self-esteem. Do I use my looks to get what I want? No. That's superficial and couldn't be further from my personality." I skip a few stones to tamper down my frustration that she would even think such a thing. "Anyone that gets to know me sees me as loyal, caring, and friendly with everyone. Looks or possessions should never play a part in how you treat someone. That's in part why I'm so nice to Madison. If you pull back your own bias, you'll see she needs friends just like anybody else."

"I don't care who you're friends with," she says, paying more attention to her rocks than me. "We're fine. No awkwardness," she assures. She skips the rocks in rapid succession.

I don't believe her. The tension in her face could be mistaken as concentration, but I'm good at reading people. She's trying not to let me see what she's holding back.

"I'm sorry I didn't pick you up to hang out like I

mentioned yesterday. I wasn't sure if you'd still want to. You were pretty distant and snarky last night."

"No biggie," she says as she takes a seat on the ground. I take a seat next to her.

"So when did you find out you were adopted?" I ask, changing the subject. I think this is part of what she's suppressing—where her some of her underlying mistrust of others stems from.

"Jan and Steve waited until I was leaving for college."

"Why do you call them that instead of Mom and Dad?"

"Because they're not my real parents. I'm not mad anymore, but it still hurts to know that I wasn't wanted."

She looks straight ahead, but I see the break in her armor. She is hurting and pushes people away before they get too close and leave. I'm not sure if my empath ability is another one of my powers, but it has always been a part of who I am.

"Let me ask you something. Have Jan and Steve provided a good home for you, shown you love, and raised you to be a good person?"

"Yes, but—"

"Then there are no buts. Biology has nothing to with it. They are your parents. They love you, and it's unfair to punish the people who did choose you. Not every parent gives their child up for adoption due to lack of love ... it's one of the most unselfish things a person can do if they know they can't give you the life and support you deserve.

Jan and Steve didn't have to choose you, but they did. They deserve all your love and gratitude."

Her head drops, and she nods. "I guess I'd been so caught up in my own feelings that I didn't stop to think about how they must feel. It's not that I'm unappreciative. I love them. I was just upset that they waited so long to tell me. My whole life felt like a lie and now to learn about all of this."

"Maybe they were waiting for a sign that you could handle it because from what you've shared, it doesn't seem like you took the news well. Our lives are what we make them. This bit of supernatural news is a game changer for sure, but we'll acclimate and prevail."

She smiles over at me, but it doesn't reach her eyes. "So what about you? Any guesses as to which parent may not be biological?"

"That's just it. Regardless of what all of this reveals, they're still my folks no matter what. One of them or neither could be biological, but I don't care. DNA shouldn't be the only criteria to call yourself a parent. And I would never call them by their first names. That's beyond disrespectful."

"Well, apparently I'm just a judgmental, disrespectful, unappreciative brat," she responds, a slight tremble in her voice giving away her hurt.

"Don't say those things about yourself. We all have room for growth, including me. Sometimes we just need to hear another people's perspective. Next time you talk with them, try calling them Mom and Dad. Watch how much better you feel and how happy you'll make them."

"I want to see them next time we go out," she confesses. "But it will always be so late. How do I explain wanting to visit them so late?"

My eyes bulge, and words fail me. I point at the ground next to her until her eyes follow my finger. She gasps, clearly shocked as me. I pick up the crystal looking unicorn she just made with a twirl of her fingers.

"Did I do that?" she asks, stunned as I hold the iced figurine between us.

"Yes, but how?"

"I don't know. It's ice," she remarks as she examines her masterpiece. "I was just thinking about the crystal figurines that my parents would give me for each birthday. Last year, it was a unicorn, and it's back in my dorm."

"This is amazing. So detailed. Let's keep this little discovery between us for now," I suggest.

"Oh, for sure. I'm not exactly ready to be part of the exhibit for show and tell. I don't even know if I could do that again."

"Why did you tell everyone what we were?" I question. I've been wanting to ask as soon as we were away from the others.

"Honestly, I don't know. I wanted to take away the opportunity for you to tell them, I guess. It was stupid."

"Well, the cat is out of the bag now. The group promises not to share, but that's not very realistic. It only takes one person to spill."

"I truly am sorry. I wish I could take it back."

"It's out there now, so let's not dwell on it. Can I get you another beer?"

"Nah. I think I'm going to head back and get ready for what awaits us tomorrow. Thanks for the chat."

"Yeah. I think we both needed that. Let me take you back on Shelby." I help her to her feet. "I insist."

When we get back to the campfire, it's as though we never left. The side conversations continue, so I'm guessing the entertainment portion of the evening is over. Madison's eyes narrow, but she stays quiet. I inform the group that I was taking Genesis back to her dorm. Some acknowledge, and some are too immersed in their own discussions. We arrive back at the dorm, and Genesis invites me in for tea. I'm not ready to say goodbye yet either, but I know I need to pump the brakes. We just made progress with our friendship. I decline her offer and promise her another time.

CHAPTER THIRTEEN

Genesis

Classes have been enlightening thus far. After finally getting our uniforms, I was pleased that it looked nothing like the plaid stereotypical schoolgirl crap Madison wears. Elysian's uniform is just black leather-like jeans with a white neoprene-type tank. My uniform complements his but is a little more involved. The black top resembles a Kevlar tactical vest. Straps and buckles hug my black, jean-clad thighs. I even have matching arm cuffs from the elbow down. I feel so badass. Elysian joked that it looked more like I was going to battle than to class, but it was explained that the clothing was a strategic choice. It aids in the regulation of our respective body temps, thus reducing accidental use of our powers from temperature surges. Stress causes the surge, and the surge causes us to unleash our powers without warning.

. . .

After being outfitted with the uniforms for our classification, we get our schedules. We started with Supernatural Analogies 101. The focus is on the capabilities of each supernatural being with an understanding that not every person reaches their greatest potential. Some powers are more readily accessible than others, and it takes practice and consistency to coax out the more advanced abilities. I was intrigued to learn that demigods and demigoddess share a foundation of increased speed, agility, and strength. But in addition to this, we possess our own unique powers such as fire and ice manipulation. Well, as Professor Thorne explained in more technical terms, one of my powers is glaciokinesis, and Elysian has the power of ignikinesis, which basically means the same as fire and ice manipulation.

Next, we had our Managing Expectations class. The jest is that each course has a theory and application component. The practice of our powers is meant to be confined to these courses and with supervision. *Too late.* Last night's gathering already broke that rule. The rules for the academy are too numerous to remember, so we are given a handbook for reference. This leads into the rules for our existence. Non-negotiable rules set forth by Earth's council, which is similar to Earth's political structure except humans are ignorant of our rules. They don't know that supernaturals exist. Three guiding principles are at the forefront of these rules.

. . .

"Rules are in place by *'The Council,'* which is made up of two supernatural beings from every class found on Earth to ensure compliance and harmony among the supernatural and human race. It is important that supernatural existence is concealed to prevent fear, chaos, and war," Professor Thorne emphasizes. "Broken rules have a punishment system in place similar to the human judicial system. There is a supernatural jail and prison, but the more extreme offenses are punishable through banishment. These rules are at the core of most rules.

Rules:

1. Supernaturals must conceal one's own identity class and/or the existence of any supernatural being.
2. Don't use supernatural powers in the presence of humans.
3. Don't use supernatural powers for personal gain, to harm, or create an unfair advantage against humans.

After lunch, we have study hour to work on stuff from our individual universities followed by a Social Norms class that is a type of psych course.

. . .

"What do you feel like eating, princess?" Elysian taunts.

"I'm not a princess ... and you can pick."

"You're the vegan in this friendship," he insists. His talent for reminding me that we're just friends is not very inconspicuous.

"Vegetarian, I correct."

"Well, pardon me. Still, you're the one with the special diet. I'll eat anything."

I try to contain my grin, but it's futile. I double over in laughter while he just stares at me incredulously.

"Did you just have a dirty thought?" I shake my head furiously, but he's not buying it. "You did too. The moment I said I'll eat anything, you broke out into a fit of hysterics. You dirty girl."

. . .

"Hush it."

"What good does it do for me to keep my innuendos to myself if you're just going create your own?"

"Food. Let's get back to food," I suggest, drying the tears from my eyes. "Besides, I'm not the dirty one. I'm sweet."

"I bet you are." His eyes darken for a split second, but I saw it. "Back to the food," he agrees.

"That curry stuff you brought to the creek Saturday was pretty tasty."

"It's settled then. I'll take you."

He really is thoughtful and kind like he spoke about last night. It makes sense that I'm starting to crush on him a bit. Okay, maybe more than a bit. It's the real reason I get so flustered when I see him with Madison. She can have any guy here, so why can't she just go pick one of them? Elysian is connected with me and not her.

. . .

"So tell me about Shelby. How did the two of you meet?" His steps falter. "Or not. I understand if she's a sore subject."

"No. It's fine. You just surprised me is all." We continue to walk toward the restaurant. "We met our freshman year in biology. It was your stereotypical guy-meets-girl moment. She was the nerd, and I was the jock in the story even though I told you I don't describe myself as being one. I pretended to need her to tutor me. Science is my favorite subject ... I probably could have tutored her. Anyway, it worked. All the long study hours together afforded her to get to know the real me and not the jock everyone assumes that I am."

I swallow my guilt because I'm everyone. "What happened?"

"Graduation happened. As we began our final stretch toward graduation, she started having doubts about us. It should have been a red flag that she kept me a secret from her parents. I wasn't who they'd pictured for her. I didn't care how opposite we were ... it's what made her special. She said we needed a break to see if we were both just settling for what was comfortable. That break was for her because I didn't have any doubts."

. . .

"Maybe you'll get back together." He and I may be connected, but it's clear she still has his heart.

"I'm done waiting. I heard that she is in another relationship now—a quiet, nerdy guy from the debate team who's more her speed and fit her parents' expectations. All I can do is pick up the pieces that were my life before she stormed into it."

"I'm sorry. Maybe I shouldn't have brought her up."

"No problem. Talking about it is good. It makes it more real. I'm getting ready to start a new chapter in my life that she won't be a part of. Anyway, what about you? When was your last boyfriend?"

"I did have a boyfriend. We broke up the day I got brought here."

"Uh-oh. What happened?"

. . .

"It was nothing like what you had with Shelby. We were only together for six months. Before then, I kept my head down and focused on my studies. I had a small group of friends that he kind of worked his way into. He was the artsy, creative type. One night, we got separated from our mutual friends, and we just kind of hit it off."

"So what went wrong?"

"He started to change. First, he joined a frat house, which was no big deal. But then he morphed into someone I didn't recognize. His partying and quest for popularity was a turn-off, and we started to grow apart. When all this weird stuff started happening with me, I couldn't tell him, so I avoided him. He read it as me blowing him off and keeping things from him, so he broke it off with me. It was a long time coming, so it didn't hurt as much. Nothing like your story."

"Well, we both have some healing to do. And I will say I'm glad that I don't have to start this next chapter alone. It's great to have a partner in this mess—someone who gets it."

"Same," I agree.

QUANTUM ENTANGLEMENT: PART ONE

⌅

"So, what's up with you and the demigod hottie now?" Loren probes. "You can't keep telling me it's nothing."

"It is nothing. We're just friends," I insist as I set up a blanket and several pillows on the floor facing my 42" television. Elysian is due to arrive at any minute.

"Friends, huh? What's this setup you have going on? It looks like a date night to me."

"Elysian is coming over, but it's not what you think. We both like the shows *I Dream of Jeannie* and *Bewitched,* so we planned a little television marathon."

I spread a variety of candy in the middle of the blanket just as the microwave dings to let me know the popcorn is ready.

"Sure thing. I think you're both in denial, but it's not my business." She walks over to her side of the closet and begins to rummage through a basket of folded clothes. "Here is my contribution to your *date*."

. . .

She hands me a bottle of Jack Daniel's. "It's not a date." I sigh as I take the liquor from her.

"Mhmm. Well, while the two of you have your *non-date* night, I'm going to hang with a few girls you haven't met yet. They're from my coven. They're super chill, so we'll have to all get together soon."

"You're welcome to stay."

"Not a chance. Thanks for the invite, but I'll pass."

The sound of three rapid knocks has my heart slamming against my chest. Why was I suddenly nervous? This isn't a date. We're just two friends hanging out. I blow out a cleansing breath and ignore the accusatory stare I'm getting from Loren. I go to the door and pull it open just as Elysian is about to knock again.

"I see you're breaking out the big guns," he jokes, gesturing toward the whiskey still in my hand.

. . .

"Ummm ... Loren just gave this to me from her secret stash."

"Good evening, Loren. Will you be joining us for our Nick at Nite marathon?"

Oh, jeez. I brace myself for her inference that this is more than what it is. Please don't say the *date* word.

"Nah. You two kids have fun. I have other plans tonight."

That's it? Thank goodness. I guess she has more restraint than I gave her credit for.

"Have fun with the girls," I say as she heads toward the door.

"He looks mighty fucking yummy. You better get on that before Madison seals the deal. It's not like she hasn't been trying," she whispers in my ear. She then smiles at us both, leaving a flush of crimson on my face.

If he heard her, he isn't letting on that he did. He takes a seat on the blanket and looks through all the candy. If I'm being honest, he does look insanely hot. His shirt clings to his chest and abs with every swoon-worthy etch of perfection on display. His gym shorts hug his muscled thighs, providing ideas about how powerful his thrusts must be. He flips his shoulder-length hair as his cerulean blue eyes pierce mine. The skeleton key he always wears dangles around his neck.

"Are you just going to stand there staring at me, or are you ready to get this marathon started?" he teases.

"I'm not staring at you. I'm looking at the key you never take off. What is it for?" Nice save, if I say so myself.

"Yes, you were. But it's okay. I've already accepted that you're a little weird."

"Shut it," I respond, embarrassed that I got caught and wasn't as crafty with my excuse as I thought. Luckily, he can't read my thoughts.

"I've had this key as long as I remember. Even as a kid. When I asked my folks about it, they had no clue other than I was attached to it. As long as nobody was missing it, they didn't see the harm. Now it's part of what makes me ... well me, so I never take it off."

Everybody has their quirks, I guess. I don't question him anymore about the key. I grab the popcorn from the microwave and then take a seat next to him. I snatch the Almond Joy from the pile, and he gives me the side-eye.

"I don't even like those." He grins. "I'll happily take the Sour Patch. Where are your cups?"

I point him in the direction of our mini fridge. We don't have many dishes, but the few we do have are enough for two people. He gets up, and it takes everything in me not to stare. I blame Loren. Why did she have to go and make me see just how sexy he is? I mean, it's hard to miss, but damn. I busy myself with changing the channel to *Bewitched*. Sam wiggles her nose to move something across the room, and the irony is not lost on me that unlike the witch she is playing on TV, they actually exist. My roommate is a witch. I have to remember to ask her if she can move things with a wiggle of her nose.

"So you're just going to start the show without me? Some

host you are."

"This episode is almost over. To be honest, I've seen most of them. I just like watching them all over again."

"Oh, absolutely. That's part of the fun."

He sits back down next to me, closer than he was before. I can feel the heat radiate from his skin, and my nerves are back. He pours the whiskey into the cups he filled with Coke and passes one to me. I happily accept. Anything to take the edge off. He looks at me with a raised eyebrow.

"What?" Why was he looking at me like that? Studying me. "Who's staring now?" I tease as I shove him.

"You know, you're kind of cute," he surmises.

Where in the hell did that come from? "Wait. Only kind of?" I try to make a joke so he doesn't see the butterflies he's stirring inside me. The feeling is so foreign. I didn't even feel this with Cooper.

. . .

"You know that you're cute. But I get to see you this way."
He wiggles his eyebrows.

"What way?" He now has my undivided attention.

"This carefree redhead with a tank that can barely
support her boobs and cheer shorts that show off lean but
muscular legs. Oh, and your top bun is so adorable. It's
such a contradiction to your effortless sex appeal."

I take his cup and peer down at its contents. Yup, still
full. "Okay. What did you drink or pop before you came
here?"

"Pop?"

"You know. Like popping pills."

"Actually, I don't know. I don't pop pills. Hell, before I
came to this academy, I didn't even drink this much. My
life was wrestling and working with my team to win the

championship again." He tugs at my top knot, and I feel a throb inside my panties. Ugh, it's not like he said anything too suggestive. He's looking at me too close now. I blame the lack of attention my vagina has gotten lately. "So why is it when I tell you how sexy you look right now without even trying, your first thought is that I've taken something?"

"Well, because I know you don't look at me that way. We're just friends."

"We are friends, but that doesn't mean that my eyes don't work. I was just thinking about how I'm the only one that gets a front row seat to just how sexy you really are. Now we can get back to the show."

How in the hell am I supposed to concentrate on the TV show now that he has dropped that whole *"you're sexy"* bomb? I take a few hearty gulps of my whiskey. The accompanying burn is a good indication that there is more alcohol than soda in this cup.

"You know, you're pretty heavy-handed there with the alcohol," I accuse.

. . .

"You only had one Coke left. I had to split it between both of our cups."

"We have several cans of Sprite left and even more of sparkling water," I point out.

"Umm, no. You don't mix either of those with whiskey." He takes a sip of his own Coke-deprived concoction. "You just remember to sip yours. You know your tolerance isn't that of a normal person."

I take a few more gulps in spite. "Too late. My cup is empty. I think I need a refill."

"Any more and you'll be smashed before the next episode of *Bewitched* starts." He passes me the popcorn instead. I roll my eyes but take the bag anyway. The alcohol has done absolutely nothing to dull the ache between my legs —if anything, it's intensified.

The show starts, and soon, we're in hysterics over Samantha's and Darren's antics. The reprieve of sexual tension is rewarding. We watch so many episodes that I don't remember the moment my head rested against Elysian's shoulder. He looks down at me at the precise moment that I look up at him. I feel his kinetic energy pulling me closer. His lips brush against mine softly, and just like that, those damn butterflies are back. And they brought back the tingling to my lady bits. I don't have the strength to put the brakes on this not so friendly exchange even if I wanted to. My tongue darts out and lick the seam of his lips. A guttural growl escapes him as he opens for me. He deepens the kiss hungrily. His hands entwine deep within my hair, fisting the strands around his grip. My head falls back as a soft, audible moan slips past my lips, but he continues his assault along my neck. The ache between my legs grows so exponentially that clenching my pelvic floor muscles are futile. The moment a single hand palms my ass, the rest of my composure comes undone. I begin to tug at his shirt, urging him to take it off.

"Shit," he curses underneath his breath. "We can't do this. This was a mistake," he says, standing quickly to his feet.

"Right," I agree. I'm such an idiot.

"Sorry," he offers.

"It's fine. You're right. This was a mistake. This whole

night was a fucking mistake."

I jump up and begin to clean up the remaining snacks lying about. I can't even look at him after I just made an ass out of myself.

"Let me help," he offers, picking up the empty bag of popcorn.

"Just go," I snap, yanking the bag from his hand. "I'll take care of this mess. Please," I add a little softer.

His eyes soften, and he looks like he wants to say more, but he doesn't. Instead, he leaves out the door without a backward glance.

That went south fast. My pride is more than a little wounded. Damn, he had to feel that. He kissed me back. He said he was ready to move on from his ex. Did he have a change of heart, or does he have his sights set on someone more his speed? Someone like Madison. *Ugh*. None of my business. He wants to be strictly friends? *Noted*. I won't make that mistake again.

CHAPTER FOURTEEN

Elysian

My eyelids struggle to open, but the noise from outside is too loud to allow me to sleep. I grumble noises under my breath. They clearly weren't anything close to actual words because none of it made any sense in my own head. I finally pull the curtain to see what's happening outside so early, and to my disbelief, a class was already in session out in the yard. This can't be ... classes don't begin till nine a.m. today. At least to my understanding. I found my phone mixed up in the middle of my sheets. I must have fell asleep with it. I usually have it on the nightstand plugged in at night. The screen lights up, and the first thing I see is a big 9:07. I panic for a split second because there is no way. My alarm hasn't even gone off yet. I give it a harder thought now that my brain is more alert at the moment.

Shit!

I remember being on the phone late last night trying to clear my mind from things that happened earlier, and I definitely forgot to set the alarm before my body was sent into a coma-like sleep. I rush to fling on the lame school uniform. Without any time to eat or brush my teeth, this is just going to have to do for now. Racing through the halls, I wonder if it is going to be awkward to see Genesis. Gosh, I hope not. I don't think she would be that type of girl to make a big deal about it. If anything, she's the type to hold things in. I need to keep these thoughts out of my mind. There are more important things to think about currently. Like one, getting my ass to class. This is the one class I have with other students and not just her and I. She's not in this class at all.

I work my way stealthy out to the schoolyard to merge with the rest of the students. I'm only twenty minutes late, so I couldn't have missed too much. There are another forty minutes left. Pleased I made it in without any embarrassing attention for arriving late, I tap the kid next to me.

"Hey, man, what has happened so far? I accidentally slept in."

"You're good, dude. He has just been explaining some stuff about practicing skills and safety. Generic stuff that applies to all magic."

"Alexo!" a loud voice calls from the front.

"Yes, Professor Richey?" he replies.

"Please tell me that you're catching Elysian up to date on what he has missed for being late to class. I would hate to have to repeat myself." The professor clearly saw him join the rest of the class late.

"Yes, sir. He is ready for today."

"Alright, that is what I like to hear. For everyone, allow us to finish covering some safety and boundary information before we begin to test our gifts with a partner. Elysian, I would like to see you after class. Alrighty then, let us get started."

As the class continues, we break into partners, and I jump in with Alexo. Everyone seems to have a decent grasp on their gift or power, and each one is not like the rest. Everyone is so different. They are all so incredible. Not to mention Alexo's ability to harden his body. His skin seems to legit transform into a substance so tough and impenetrable it's practically metal. He's a warlock. He explains it's an illusion spell that makes the shield he's holding look like it's a part of him. He's going to be so badass. Sucks that I can't even figure out how to access my own power... fire. And I'm a demigod ... supposedly. I sure don't feel like one. Even with my impressive strength, I'm not nearly as talented as the rest of these guys. From all my tests, they say I can create fire, and I've struggled all class period with nothing to show for it. Not even a puff of smoke. I don't even know that I felt warm. But I can't give up. There has to be a reason I have this power and a reason I was born in the first place. I don't know what that is yet, but when that time comes, I do not want to let anyone down. Like what if the world is at stake?

"Elysian," Professor Richey calls for my attention.

I quickly turn. "Yes, sir."

"Come over here when you are done daydreaming."

That's right. He wanted me to stay after, and class is just ending. All because I was late this morning. Now I have to sit here longer and listen to some speech about being more responsible and on time. I say my goodbyes to my classmates and head in his direction.

"I hope you understand why I'm keeping you after," the professor starts.

"It either has to do with me being tardy or that I suck as a student here."

He laughs. "Oh no, neither of those are any of my concerns. I already know that you will have difficulty learning your fire power. And there's a reason for that. You are too much of an optimist."

"And that is bad?" I question with confusion. "And I prefer to think that I'm a realist."

"In this specific case, yes, it is. You see, the ability to bring forth fire is mostly derived from pain and anger. Fire is an incredible force, one that must be taken seriously because it destroys everything in its path. And because of this, you must learn to control it. Fire is power, but without full control, you can hurt someone."

"I can understand that."

"This is the moment your journey truly begins, Elysian. And it will be the toughest journey anyone will have to go through. You will be tested and forced to dig into some dark moments of your life, and then while you are there, it is imperative for you to learn to become absolutely calm with your emotions. Only then will you develop complete control."

"Uhhh, okay." I respond without actually understanding what he means.

"I need you to think back to a time that caused you excruciating pain."

"But sir, I don't think anything like that has ever happened to me."

"Close your eyes and clear your mind. Don't think about responding to me. Inside yourself, you need to open the book of your own life, flip through the years, and find the good times."

I see so much love from my parents and friends. They were always there to support me at my games and gave me all the opportunities a boy could want. My dad taught me how to be a young man he was proud of.

"Now, between those moments, remember the bad times. All the way throughout your childhood and teen years."

Ah yes, some kids would pick on me because I was different. I always went along with their jokes and laughed too. I remember the pain from sledding one year where I hit a tree and broke my arm. I remember not being allowed to be in the play at my school in fifth grade.

"Dig deeper," he encourages, reading my mind. "Bring back a moment that was so painful you repressed it completely and ended up believing it never existed. A moment that you made disappear as if it never actually happened."

I do what he asks of me. I close my eyes and think as hard as I can, but nothing comes to mind. My brain jumps through all my years. Was there possibly something? I just don't know ... I've lived a fairly good life.

"You need to remember; you need to find what your heart longed for the most, Elysian."

And there is was! It hit me like a fucking train. My heart sank into a bottomless pit, my body shaking uncontrollably ... my breath panicked, short and choppy.

"Nooooo!" The word explodes out of me. "I don't want this."

"Don't let it go. You must harness this feeling, kid."

The pain is overwhelming. As I pour sweat, I strive to keep it close. Like a wick, the center of my chest is a burning flame. Suddenly, I open my eyes, and he tells me that they're glowing red.

"Yes, Elysian, you did it!" Professor Richey cheers with excitement.

But I don't know how excited he should be. I have this overwhelming rage swirling through my bones. My skin feels like it's on fire, and I feel different. The only thing I desire right now is to kill. Kill everything around me.

"Professor! You need to leave right now," a thunderous voice comes out from inside me.

"I can't do that; I am here to help you! You need to ease your emotions in the state you are in. Remember the pain but allow the anger to simmer away!" He continues to yell at me. "Fire that is produced from anger is wild, but fire that emerges from understanding is yours to control."

"I can't do that, though!" I scream again. "It was all my fault! I am the one to blame."

"Elysian, listen to me! You need to let it go. To forgive yourself because it wasn't your fault. You were just a child. You need to find peace."

"But how? How do I do that?" The enormous power radiating from me pushes back the professor even farther.

"I know it hurts, and it seems impossible to get past. But you will only be hurting yourself if you do not try to move forward. Your true potential will never be realized. Accept what happened and release yourself from it all."

I bring the pain back to the center of my body. Isolating the presence it has within me. I grit my teeth and dig my toes into the ground, holding onto all the confidence I can muster. It seems as if things are getting easier or maybe I am just adapting to it. It was so long ago, but how did I not remember at first. I have to believe it is best to let go. What good am I doing to myself? To anyone? People depend on me. I do not want anyone else that I love to ever get hurt again!

The world goes silent.

I look down at myself, body no longer tense. I'm warm, but I don't feel like I am going to explode. I look back up at my professor. He confirms that my eyes are no longer bright red but maintain a slight glow to them.

"Well done, kid! Well done!" He claps with enthusiasm. "Now, open your palm and create a flame."

I raise my clenched fist and slowly open my fingers, palm toward the sky. Channeling my mind to the middle of my hand, I send all my heat there, and a floating ball of orange appears. Controlled in my hand. I have fire. I did it.

"Terrific. You conquered your fear, and you just made your biggest step to becoming something absolutely amazing, Elysian. Now release that feeling inside you, and lower your body temperature back to normal."

I do just that, and everything returns to the way they were.

"Whoa, that was wild." I collect my thoughts. "Thank you so much for everything, Professor Richey. You have helped so much more than you know."

"You are welcome, kid. You will continue to grow your control and ability, and I will be right beside you to help. Now, you must be exhausted. Go get some lunch and rest. You have more classes to attend later."

"Yes sir, will do. Thank you again."

I have so many questions for my parents now that I know I was adopted too. I'm not upset. They've given me the best life. I need to talk to Genesis first. I need to tell her what I've discovered today and show her that I can now access my fire power. We're more alike than we both thought. But first, we'll have to get through the possible tension and awkwardness of last night's kiss.

CHAPTER FIFTEEN

Genesis

I throw my book bag to the floor and flop onto my bed. Today has been an exhausting mind fuck. Class today poured salt all over my wounded pride. I had to endure watching Elysian make progress with his ability to produce and manipulate fire at will while I failed over and over again at any attempt to summon any of mine. Professor kept coaching me to relax and concentrate, to allow meditation to clear whatever was blocking my abilities. Unbeknownst to him, that blockage was a person, and he had a front row seat to my repeated failure. The tension between us was palpable, and the pity reflected in his eyes made me nauseous. He was at least concerned over how our night ended.

"There you are. How did last night go?" Loren asks as she slams the door behind her. Talk about timing. The salt just keeps pouring. "You were asleep when I came in last night, so I missed getting the deets."

"Well, you didn't miss much," I deadpan. "It was a disaster."

"Oh, no. What happened?"

I force myself to sit up and face her. She's the one that help put the crazy notion in my head that things between Elysian and I can be more than platonic.

"You want the CliffsNotes version?"

"If that's what you prefer," she agrees, nonchalantly.

"I kissed him. He kissed me back before realizing his mistake but then rejected me. His exact words were that the kiss was a mistake." I wait for her to say I told you so —that she knew I had more than friendly feelings for him and that last night was indeed a date. To my surprise, she doesn't say any of those things.

"Maybe he just wants to take things slow," she ponders, now sitting on her bed across from me.

"No. And you have to stop doing that." I breathe out a frustrating breath.

"Doing what?"

"Pushing for something that not going to happen. I'm clearly not his type. Because of you, I started seeing him as this sexy, virile man instead of the unattainable guy out of my league."

She rolls her eyes before coming to stand directly in front of me. "First of all, your eyes work. You didn't need me to point out just how hot he is. Second, he kissed you back. It takes two to tango. My guess is that he is in denial same as you. If he's holding back, it's not because he's out of your league. Have you looked in a mirror? You're stunning."

Now it's my turn to roll my eyes. "Well, to add insult to injury, I totally looked inferior today in class. He is already progressing while my powers are starting to look like a fluke."

I tell her about today and how each class made me feel like an utter failure.

"I'm not surprised. Not by the failure part, but the inability to summon your abilities. You have to learn how to channel all that power, and it takes focus. Nothing at that moment should matter but the power you're conjuring. You possess powers, but if you're distracted, it will cause blockage. That's why you're here—to learn."

"Honestly, I'm starting to doubt all of this. What's the point? I wish I could go back to my old life where things made sense. Unseen and unbothered."

"Things will get better. With or without him, you will be the best damn demigoddess there is. This isn't a race to see who can harness their abilities the fastest. Your powers will appear when you're ready."

"That's the thing. I don't know if I'll ever be. How can I keep putting myself through repeated defeat yet manage to maintain optimism?"

She sighs, worry creasing her brows. "I think I may be able to help, but you have to promise you won't tell anyone. Not even Elysian."

"Why would I tell him anything? He's the reason for my blockage and self-doubt. I have to face him every day, knowing I don't measure up to his abilities or his ideal woman."

"Fine. Come on," she insists as she pulls me to my feet.

I follow her out of the room, her strides eating up the pavement once we're outside. She doesn't speak a single word until we reach the campus library.

"The library?" I quirk an eyebrow at her.

She doesn't waste time with a response. She takes the elevator to the top floor with me on her heels. The floor is unoccupied. She disappears around a stack of books before reappearing again. She holds out a hand full of papers. She leads me to one of the study rooms before pushing out a piece of carved drywall. Hidden are several artifacts that I'm unfamiliar with.

"What's all of this?" I ask as she sifts through the copies.

"These are spells," she admits. "I copied them from the Grimoire."

"You have the Grimoire?" I ask a little too loudly. She puts her hand over my mouth to shush me, looking around to confirm we're truly alone.

"I don't have it but know where it is. My uncle doesn't know that I know. I didn't have time to review it in its entirety, so I stole it long enough to make a few copies before returning it."

"What spells did you copy, and what's all this other stuff for?"

Twine, a compass, a granite mortar and pestle, and a

small zip bags of herbs are among the individual items spread out on one of the study tables.

"I have a spell in here to help you focus and concentrate on what it is that you want. This should allow you to better access your abilities. A few of the things on the table are needed to conduct the spell."

"Okay," I agree. I have my doubts, but I don't voice them. She took a big risk showing me all of this. Besides, she's the one that found a way for us to sneak off campus, so she clearly has a handle on this kind of stuff.

I watch as she reads from the paper and mixes herbs in the mortar, using some unknown liquid as the wetting agent. After a paste forms, she spreads it onto my left inner wrist where my branding lies dormant underneath my skin.

"Just let that dry and infuse into your skin overnight," she remarks while putting everything back into its hiding place.

"Do you have to chant something for it to work?" I ask.

"Nope. No incantation needed. The magic is in the poultice."

"Thank you," I say as we head back to our dorm.

There is only a hint of daylight left, so I'm guessing it's almost nine. A soak in the tub after today's assault sounds inviting. I need to make sure I don't get my wrist wet. I can feel the tingle underneath the surface of my skin although I don't feel any more focused than usual. We arrive back at our dorm after a brief walk. Loren pauses in the doorway, her step faltering.

"How did you get in here?"

This piques my interest. I look around her to see Elysian sitting on my bed. "Sorry. Your door was cracked, and it opened when I knocked. I came in figuring you wouldn't be gone long if you left your door open. Just needed to talk to Genesis."

"Didn't realize we left it open," Loren admits. She looks back and forth between Elysian and me. "I'm going to go pay Bethany a visit. It's almost time for curfew, so keep your voices down."

When she looks at me one more time, I can't read her subliminal eyebrow wagging, but it doesn't take much to guess. I close the door behind her. I look over at Elysian who hasn't moved from my bed. He's wearing more of his fitted gym shorts and tank— not what he was wearing earlier. I have to tear my gaze away from his muscled thighs. This man told me kissing me was a mistake. I'd do well to remember that.

I walk over to him with my arms folded. "What did you need to talk with me about?"

He stands and hovers above me, and my bravado weakens. I inhale his fresh scent, and my clit pulsates.

"I'm done with pretending," he announces, successfully catching me off guard. "Do you want me?"

"What? W-Where is this c-coming from?" I stutter.

"Answer the question, Genesis. Tell me the truth."

"I don't want anything. The kiss was a mistake, remember?"

"Ummmm. I remember that lie. That kiss was anything but a mistake, and I think we both know that." He takes a step closer, and my breath becomes labored. "I'm going to ask again. Do you want me? Want this?"

His hand grabs mine and places it firmly against his hard cock. The fabric of his shorts leaves nothing to imagine. "Fuck me."

"Is that what you want, babe?"

I didn't even realize I said that out loud. My panties flood with desire. This can't be happening. "If this is some sort of sick joke, it's not funny," I reply, my voice still a tremor.

"Does the hardness of my cock seem like a joke? Say the word and I'll show you just how serious I am. I'm done denying myself what I've wanted from the moment I laid eyes on you."

I grab the side of his tank, but words fail me. I want to let go and let him do all the things his gorgeous blues are silently promising me. He turns us so that the back of my knees hits the bed. I sit on the bed, and his protruding hardness is now in my direct sight.

"If this is not what you want, tell me now, sweetheart."

I swallow the lump in my throat. I'm speechless. I want him inside me. Consequences be damned. All of our denial has led up to this moment. If I only get this one night with him, so be it.

"Okay then," he says with finality, making my silence

as his cue to continue. He crawls onto my bed over me with sheer determination. I watch as he pulls his T-shirt over his head. *Sweet baby Jesus ... this is really happening.* I tremble slightly at the thought. He grips my inner thighs before pulling me down closer to him. I lie flat on my back as he grips my gym shorts on both sides. I can only hope that Loren doesn't come back anytime soon.

"Lift," he commands. His voice is thick, rough, and dominant. He's still Elysian but different somehow. I lift my hips as instructed. He pulls my shorts and panties down to my knees with one pull. "Last chance, Genesis. No regrets."

"No regrets," I whisper. That is all the reassurance he needs to yank my shorts and panties the remaining way off.

"I can smell how fucking wet you are for me," he says, his face hovering over my pussy. I cover my eyes with my hands. "No hiding from what we both want, baby. I'm going to worship this pussy and fulfill all the fantasies we've both been denying ourselves," he vows.

The vulgar promises he spews make me even wetter. This feeling ... this moment ... I never want it to end. He sits me up partially so he can remove my tank and then my bra. When he has all of my clothes off, I'm naked in every aspect of the word. I hope he knows that I'm giving myself to him in every way—more than just with my body. Though I'm not a virgin, I've never been this comfortable in my own skin. This vulnerable. The feeling is indescribable. He swings my legs so that they're both on the bed before laying me on my back once again. He brings his body down on top of mine, and I shiver with anticipation. We're chest to chest and the heat from the contact is scorching. He gives me a wicked smile before bringing his lips to meet mine. This kiss is so soft, unlike the unbridled passion of our first kiss that he deemed a mistake. Our tongues slowly meet in a sensual dance that builds the ache between my thighs to new soaring heights.

He parts my legs with one of his muscular thighs, and I rub myself against him, desperate for friction. He deepens the kiss while grinding against me. I swear I can come from his kiss and dry humping alone. He nips at my lips and immediately licks away the pain. My body trembles now for a different reason other than anticipation.

"Hmmm. Patience, love." He plants gentle kisses along my neck before following a trail down to my breast. He gives them each attention with just the right amount of licking and nibbling. So, I see he is a nibbler, and it's sexy as fuck. He continues south, and I know where he's heading next. I brace myself as he takes that first lick to my clit.

"Fuuuuuck," I moan. My thighs tighten on their own accord around his head, but he isn't having it.

"Let me in." He pushes my legs apart while simultaneously sucking on my nub. He sucks, then nibbles in a frenzy so enthralling, I feel a sensation of release on the precipice. I grab his shoulder-length hair as I ride the fuck out of his face with wild abandonment. Elysian is right there with me. He pushes his tongue deep into my entrance and works me toward that orgasm my body so desperately needs. I squirt so hard my whole body shakes. He looks up at me, so proud of himself. In one quick instance, he rids himself of his gym shorts. *Damn, his package is even pretty. Hard, pink perfection.*

He takes a condom from the pocket of his shorts and slowly rolls it over his cock. He is giving me a show. And oh, what a beautiful show it is. The length and girth are intimidating, but I will take every inch. I watch on as he gives it a few strokes with his hand.

"I want your lips around my dick, but right now, I can't wait a second longer to be inside you," he admits. My legs open in invitation, and he doesn't hesitate to accept. He positions himself at my entrance and teases me with a few strokes with just the head.

"Stop teasing me," I plead.

"So greedy, my little spitfire." He winks. I'm about to object, but then he slams into me, and the words are lost on my tongue. He stills briefly, allowing me to savor his fullness. He stretches me to capacity, and it feels amazing. He eases back and slams into me again. I whimper at the heavenly assault. I claw at his back, desperate for him to go deeper. He pounds into me a few more times before alternating his thrusts with a slower grind. I'm so lost in his punishing thrust; I meet him stroke for stroke. I'm already close to the edge. Just when I can no longer hold off my impending orgasm, he changes things up. In one swift move, he flips us so that I'm on top. He puts his hands behind his head and looks at me expectantly. "My turn, sweetness."

"What?" He wants me to ride him.

"Fuck me, Genesis. Ride my dick like you own it."
Fuck, I really do want to own it.

Riding really isn't my thing since I'm not all that coordinated, but I don't hesitate to try. Unsure of how to proceed, I just do what feels good. I sit up until I'm fully mounted. I lift slightly until only the head of his dick is left inside. I alternate sliding completely down his shaft and just the tip. My pussy clenches with each stroke while my tits bounce with the rhythm. His hooded eyes tell me he is enjoying the ride. I'm on fire. I can feel myself dripping down his length. His legs tense underneath me, and his control snaps. He grabs my hips and pushes me down on his dick. He takes over, and his hips piston upward to meet mine. He is fucking me from the bottom.

"Fuck, I'm going to come," he warns. "Shiiiiiiit," he groans as he finds his release. I can feel the residual twitch of his dick as he throbs inside me. That sensation is enough for me to fall over the edge with him. I throw my head back and come all over him. I collapse on his chest, but he's not done with me. He pulls out of me and tells me to get on my knees. He slaps my ass and disposes of the used condom, then tells me to hold on. After positioning himself behind me, he nudges the tip of his cock at my pussy entrance.

"Fuuuuuuck," I moan from just the tip teasing me. Every nerve ending is on fire and desperate with need.

"I got you, babe. This dick is all yours." He smacks my ass again, and the sting makes me even wetter. *Oh, my.* He nudges me again, and I can feel him already growing hard again. "I'm going to take this sweet pussy from behind, so hold on for the ride." He pulls another condom from his shorts and rolls it down that beautiful gift of his. I look back at him, and his eyes never leave mine as he enters me from behind. He brings me to three more orgasms before the night is over. I'm deliciously sore and sated. I half expect him to gather his clothes and leave me to bask in the afterglow of the amazing sex we had, but he doesn't. He pulls the cover up over us, kisses me on the temple, and tucks me into him. My heart slams against my chest as I work to get my erratic breathing under control.

"So I found out I was adopted today," he says.

I sit up and turn to look at him. You can't just say something like that in a matter-of-fact manner.

"What? Did your parents tell you that? Did you talk to them?"

"No. Today in Professor Richey's class, he could see that something was blocking me from accessing my powers. He explained where ignikinesis is derived and how to control it. He somehow knew I was suppressing hurt and anger—that I subconsciously blamed myself for something so horrific that it was keeping me from accessing that part of myself to harness my fire power."

"What was it?"

"I'm the cause of my real mom's death. I could see it

play back like a movie. It was raining, and I was about two years old. I got out my car seat for my fire truck that had fallen to the floor. My mom turned her attention to me to try to help me back into my seat. At that exact moment, another car swerved into our lane. My mom tried to swerve to miss him, but she reacted too late. We smashed head on, and she died at the scene. I remember the fire truck arriving like the one I had. I could see the police in the ambulance. I could vividly see them zip her into a black bag. My memories skipped forward to me being brought to my new family by who I'm guessing was a social worker. It was a mystery how I survived, but they didn't know I was a child of a god. I didn't talk for a year. The key was my mom's death. I had refused to let it go. So you see, we're not so different. I'm adopted too. I still love my parents for everything they've done for me, but when we're granted our passes to go off campus, we can search for answers together."

"I'm so sorry to hear about your mom or that you had to remember what happened that way. But none of it was your fault. It was a tragedy, and you're not to blame."

"I know that now," he says. "I don't know long I would have suppressed that memory if it wasn't for Professor Richey. I needed to let go in order to access that part of myself. When I first discovered what really happened and was able to calm myself, you're the first person I wanted to tell. I just didn't want to lead with the heavy stuff tonight. I needed us to be good. I needed to erase how things ended last night."

I lie back down and snuggle into his arms, feeling even closer to him than before. I don't know what tomorrow will be bring for us, but if I don't know anything else, it's that Loren will have questions once she finds us like this. Still, I wouldn't trade this moment for any amount of questioning. I close my eyes and find solace in his arms.

CHAPTER SIXTEEN

Elysian

"Uuuhuunnn." Someone clears their throat.

I attempt to turn toward the noise, but my arm is trapped. Red flowing hair covers my arm. Seeing Genesis sleeping in my arms, I remember last night's showdown. I can't believe I threw caution to the wind and came over to satisfy what we had both been denying. And I'm still in her room and in her bed. Loren clears her throat again. This time, Genesis stirs. She rubs her eyes as we both turn to look at her friend.

"Morning," Genesis says groggily. Her naked body is still pressed against mine, and it's not helping with my morning wood.

"Don't morning me," Loren tsks. "What happened to needing to talk? And before you give me some excuse about being just friends, I can see your clothes on the floor so I know you're naked underneath those covers."

"We're all adults here," Genesis points out. She sits up and pulls the covers up around her breasts.

"Well, I'm glad you say that because I have some news you may not like."

"What is it?" I ask. I swing my legs over the bed to sit up with Genesis, careful not to give her roommate a peep show.

"Okay. Keep an open mind, guys. And just think of what I'm about to tell you as a push in the direction you both wanted to take anyway."

"Spill it," Genesis deadpans.

"Okay. You know that little spell I whipped up and rubbed into your wrist last night?"

"Go on," Genesis encourages, suspiciously.

I remember briefly seeing something on her wrist last night, but the only evidence of it now is a dry, flaky paste. There is hardly anything there.

"What spell? What was that?" I ask, turning Genesis's wrist over for a closer inspection.

Loren explains that Genesis has expressed some concern about being distracted and not being able to access her powers in class yesterday, and I'm guessing I was the distraction. She confides that she had copied some spells from the sacred Grimoire and created a poultice to spread onto Genesis to help her concentrate.

"Is there some sort of side effect? What are you not saying?" Genesis prods.

"Not exactly a side of effect," she admits. "I ran into Haley last night. She knows about the spells I stole from the Grimoire because she's the one that helps me with the reverse locator spell so we can sneak off campus. Anyway, I told her about the spell I whipped up for you." She cringes guiltily.

"And what did she say? Spit it out."

"Well, apparently the spell removes distraction and blockage by making you identify and face whatever it is you're suppressing."

"English for us, please," I speak up.

"It makes you act on whatever you've been holding back or whatever is keeping you from being able to focus. Like a truth serum or in this case ... a truth poultice. All your inhibitions were released."

"What does that even mean?" Genesis asks.

"It means your little coitus rendezvous last night was due to the poultice I spread on your wrist. It made you give in to what you wanted all along so that you could free your mind from distraction."

"I don't think so. Elysian was waiting here when we got back, remember? He brought condoms with him, so in a sense, he initiated this quote *coitus rendezvous* unquote. Yes, I may have secretly wanted it, but things wouldn't have progressed if he hadn't taken me out of the friend zone."

"Friend zone? I can assure you, you've never in that zone. My denial zone is more like it," I correct.

"You two are missing the point," Loren interrupts. "You're connected. So apparently, Genesis, you absorb his pain, but he absorbs your emotions. The minute that spell-infused poultice entered your bloodstream and heightened your emotions and desires, things were quantified for him. Elysian was motivated to carry out both his and your desires for lack of a better word. Otherwise, you may have still been in his denial zone."

"Damn." I look over at Genesis, her face solemn.

"So you really didn't want this. You were only reacting to my hidden desires," she says, trying to reach for her clothes. But I'm not having it. I pull her to me and wrap my arms around her.

"That's not what she said. Your desires quantified my own. Subconsciously, I could feel how you felt, and it gave me the encouragement to act on my own feelings. It's obvious the spell has worn off now, yet the thing I want more than anything is to get reacquainted with—"

"Oooookay," Loren interrupts. "You don't have to finish that statement. According to Kristin, he's right. If the feeling wasn't mutual, he'd simply feel your desires, but that alone wouldn't make him act on it unless he's already contemplated those same feelings in return."

"So why did you tell us? You could have kept that to yourself, and we would have never known that your little concoction moved us along toward the inevitable," Genesis questions. "Trust me, I'm not upset. I'm just curious as to why?"

"I didn't want any unsaid things hanging between us. I tried to help you last night, but moving things along between you two was the result. I came back last night and saw the two of you asleep in bed and immediately knew what Kristin told me was true. I just left and decided to wait until this morning to tell you and hoped you wouldn't be mad."

"I have to admit that last night was pretty bold on my part, and I did think I was throwing caution to the wind, but like Genesis said, I'm not mad. How could I be? Last night was amazing!"

"Ewww. TMI. Too much information." Loren fake gags.

"You know what I mean? No need to dwell on it and make it awkward."

"Well, thank you. I just came to grab a few things. I'm going to go get ready for class in Bethany's room."

We both watch as she grabs some clothes and toiletries and then heads back out the door. I push the cover back and rise to my feet. Genesis's eyes widen. It only takes a few seconds to realize that she is staring at my hard cock.

"What's that look for? It's not like you didn't get real acquainted with my dick last night."

"Ummmm. Nothing. I better get ready for class."

She gets up, ensuring to wrap the blanket around her, but I'm not letting her shy away from me. I swiftly pull her to me, yanking the blanket away with one tug. "No regrets, right? There is no spell to blame now. So, tell me."

"T-Tell you w-what?" she stutters, her breath a pant. She's either nervous or turned on. I press her bare pussy against my hardness. The slickness that I find between her legs corrects my first thought. She's both nervous and turned on.

"Tell me again that you have no regrets. Tell me how much you still want me inside you."

"No regrets," she confirms breathily. My dick slides between her legs, and she doesn't hesitate to rub herself against it.

"And? Tell me the second part. I dare you!"

"I want you inside me."

She doesn't get the rest of that sentence out. I pick her up and slam her down on my shaft. Her heat welcomes the intrusion. I walk her until her back is flush against the bathroom door. She braces for my thrust as her legs wrap tighter around my hips. She bites down on my shoulder as I fuck her with wild abandon.

"Goddammit. Your pussy is so fucking addicting ... so wet."

My hips piston faster as she continues to meet me stroke for stroke.

"It's yours. Take all of it. Fuck me harder."

The vile words coming from her sweet mouth spurs me on. Her head falls back as her pussy tightens around my dick, milking me. Our orgasms collide, and it's fucking earth shattering. I pulsate inside her until I've given her every last drop. *Shit*. I forgot to put on a condom.

"I'm on the pill," she says, looking me in the eye. She unwraps her legs and slides down my body.

"I'm clean," I promise. I never fuck without a rubber. She flinches slightly but changes the subject.

"We better get ready for class if we don't want to be late."

"Yeah. I better get going so I can shower and change. See you in class."

"Okay. Sure."

Where in the hell did this awkwardness come from all of a sudden? I could cut the tension with a knife. "Thank you for a great time, love. Wish we didn't have to get to class." I attempt to ease the tension, but it's still there.

"I had a great time too. Now you better get going." She turns to enter the bathroom and her heart-shaped ass beckons me for another round. My dick twitches in agreement. "Goodbye, Elysian," she says, closing the door.

I reluctantly throw on my clothes from last night before heading to my room. I'm careful not to be seen leaving. I don't know what any of this means or where we go from here. The sex was great, but that doesn't mean I'm ready to jump into another relationship. I don't want to put a label on anything, so I'll just have to follow her lead.

This morning's class was quite eventful. I was able to shape fire into spears and propel them out into the open. Genesis was able to make more figurines out of ice. Professor Guenther applauded us on our progress. We're learning to access our abilities on demand. He even congratulated Genesis on clearing whatever was blocking her performance. I snickered because I knew the source of the unblocking was my cock. The stern look on her face was enough for me to cut out my snickering, though.

"What's up for lunch, sweetness?" I ask, catching up to her. "Canyon's?"

"No. I want you to get what you want. I'll find something, and we can meet back here in the courtyard in thirty minutes."

"You sure?"

"Of course. Get whatever you feel like eating and meet me back here."

"Okay. See you in thirty."

I opt to skip our campus restaurants for the cafeteria. The salmon and veggies were pretty good that first day, and as luck would have it, it's on the menu again today.

"Hi there, stranger." It's Madison, and she's not alone. Two blondes in school uniform flank her sides. "I've haven't seen you since the bonfire on Sunday. How are your classes going?"

"Different than I'm used to, but I'm balancing it all," I admit.

"Hi. I'm Rachel, and this is Tonya," one of the blondes introduces.

"Nice to meet you both," I greet, shaking their hands.

"I'll catch up with you two later. I know you have to get to class," Madison dismisses. The confused look on their faces tells me that they have nowhere to be at the moment, but they wave their goodbyes anyway. "So you're eating lunch alone?" she asks, gesturing toward the container of food in my hand.

"Nah, I was actually heading to meet up with Genesis."

I take steps toward the courtyard, and she follows. "You two spend a lot of time together. Are you meeting other people? I mean besides our little group."

"Not really. This really is just the first week, so I think everyone is still getting settled into the new semester. I've gotten lots of stares, if that counts," I joke.

"I bet they've all been from women. Look at you. Don't pretend you don't know how hot you are." She bumps her shoulder against mine.

"Meh. I'm alright ... I guess."

"Alright, my ass. You could pull any girl at this academy."

"Why do I get the feeling that you're speaking about yourself?" I look over at her, and she blushes.

"And what if I am? Don't worry, I know that you're trying to get over the ex. But doesn't mean that I'm not willing and waiting for my shot. I just may need to try harder to persuade you."

"Madison ..."

"Hi, Genesis," Madison greets. I didn't even realize we had reached the courtyard.

I don't miss the disappointment etched into Genesis's face before she schools her features. "Hi," she replies flatly. She takes a seat at the nearest table, and I set my food across from her. Madison doesn't get the hint. She simply sits on the same side of the table with me.

"Are you two coming out with us Friday night?" she inquires.

"It's up to Genesis," I answer, bumping her knee underneath the table.

"Well, it would be nice to see my parents," she admits.

"It's settled then. As long as you have your same jewelry pieces, you should both be set. We'll meet at the same time as last time."

"Cool," I agree.

"How is the salmon? I always see them serving it, but I never get it," Madison asks.

It's actually really good. I go to take a bite, but she grabs my wrist and wraps her lips around my fork. "Hmmm. It is really good," she moans, her eyes never leaving mine.

"Ummm. I'm going to get going. I need to grab something from my room before our last class."

I dash in a blink of an eye before she can even get up. "You haven't eaten your food. Stay and I'll dash and get it for you."

My eyes silently plead with hers. I know she's jealous, but she has no reason to be. "I've lost my appetite. Now if you'll excuse me."

I watch as she tosses her uneaten lunch in the trash before storming off. This pisses me off. I can't control how someone else acts. Yes, Madison is blatantly coming on to me, but I haven't done anything to encourage her.

Each time, I've blocked Madison's advances by bringing her into the conversation, so why was she punishing me? I'm over it. Just because we had sex, it doesn't give her the right to expect me to jump through hoops for her.

"I don't think she likes me very much or likes me talking to you," Madison surmises. "I think she likes you."

"You have to cut the crap, Madison. We're just friends."

"Tell that to her." She laughs.

"I'm talking about us. There's nothing between us. All you're doing is purposely making her feel uncomfortable, and that's not cool. Now, I like you because I look past all your superficial bullshit, but you can't keep trying to antagonize her. I want us to all just get along."

"Whatever you say, handsome." She puts her hands up in defeat before getting up and backing away.

I don't think she plans to follow through with a damn thing I just said. That being said, I guess I should try harder to see this ordeal from Genesis's perspective. If she needs reassurance that I don't want Madison, then that's the least I can do. I won't jump through hoops, but maybe I can *unblock* her again.

CHAPTER SEVENTEEN

Elysian

O ur last class ended hours ago. As expected, Genesis was distant, giving me very little eye contact. But something was different. A heaviness in my chest. A dull ache that I finally recognized as sadness, but why? Then I remembered our connection. These weren't my feelings. They were hers. *Fuck!* I promised that I'd always have her back, even if it was from me. Gah, I'm such an idiot. She wasn't trying to make me jump through hoops. She was hurt. Did she think I was just going to move on to Madison after sleeping with her? I don't know where we go from here, but that is the last thing she should be worrying about. I pace the floor as my roommate, Brody, looks on from his bed. Shit. I can't let another minute pass without knowing the truth. I dash toward her dorm, hoping she'll let me in.

I knock a few times before Loren swings the door open. "I don't know what's going on between you two, but it sure looks like she could use another dose of whatever you served up last night."

"I just need to see her," I admit.

"She's inside the bathroom where all the sad songs are coming from. I'm out. Fix my friend."

She pushes past me, and I have my mission. The song "Bloodstream" by Stateless filters from behind the closed door. I grab the bottle of whiskey that is still sitting out from last night before easing the bathroom door open. Our eyes meet in the mirror as she pauses. Not before I catch her swaying to the beat. She's completely fucking naked and running the shower.

"Don't stop on my account," I encourage. My dick twitches against my jeans. The music is slow and climactic as it continues to play.

"Don't you have somewhere else to be ... like with Madison?"

"I'm exactly where I want to be, love. When are you going to realize I don't want Madison? I want you. Only you."

"Mhmm." She's not quite convinced.

"Tell me that you want me too, baby. I need to know. Better yet ... show me. If you want me just as much as I want you, show me the moves you were doing before I opened this door."

The lyrics are so fitting for this moment because she has gotten into my bloodstream. She slowly turns to face me, never uttering a word. Her clean-shaven pussy makes my cock jump. She gives me a shy smile before turning back around. She lets her hips begin to sway to the music once again, and I have my answer. She does want me too. I suspect not having to look at me gives her the confidence she needs to keep dancing. That's okay for now since I'm enjoying the view. The round curve of her ass has me wanting to end her little performance right now and just bury my dick deep inside her pussy.

"Turn around," I tell her after I've had enough of just seeing the back of her. I need to look in her eyes again because my dick is urging me to move this along. I take a swig of the whiskey, but it's not for me. I walk stealthily toward her. "Open." She does as I ask and opens her mouth for me. I transfer the sip of whiskey from my mouth to hers. Her eyes squint from the burn of the alcohol, but I repeat the transfer three more times. Her body relaxes with each subsequent shot of the whiskey. Her features relax, and her eyelids become hooded. I take the last shot. Our tongues dance as I transfer the liquor from my mouth to hers once again. It burns so good while I try to consume the taste of her.

"*Hmmm*," she purrs. Her hooded lids lower even farther when I trail kisses from her neck to her pebbled nipples. I think she's ready. I let my hand travel south until my fingers are slipping through her wetness.

She moves against my fingers, but I remove them. When she comes for the first time tonight, it will be on my dick and not my fingers. I lift her slowly and watch her eyes widen with surprise when she finds herself over my head—her dripping pussy in my direct line of vision. I put her legs over my shoulders and walk her to the nearest wall. When I'm sure she can't squirm too much, I bury my face between her legs. Her essence smells so damn sweet. I should have at least unzipped my jeans to give my dick room to throb. *Too late now.* My first tentative lick has her throwing her head back against the wall.

"Hold on, baby." I twirl my tongue around her clit, teasing it, worshipping it. Genesis wriggles in my arms, trying to get away from my attention. I get a tighter grip on her ass and push my face deeper. I suck on her clit with even more determination and watch as her eyes begin to roll back.

"Ely..." she mumbles incoherently. The trembling of her legs around my neck confirms that she is oh, so close. I slide my tongue through to her entrance. I slap her ass, enough to sting but not enough to cause pain. I'm diverting her focus because I don't want her coming yet. I thrust my tongue in and out of her soaking wet pussy until she is riding my face.

"That's it, baby. Ride my fucking face. Make that sweet pussy take all of my tongue."

She grinds harder, and I almost want to let her have the release she is craving right now ... almost. I lift her over my head once more to switch her in the opposite direction—the sixty-nine position. Her ass lines up with my face as her legs work to get situated behind my neck. She is facing my cock in this position. Her legs instantly wrap around my head and neck when I begin to lower her body down mine. A small gasp of air comes out in a rush from her when I let her drop to the level I need her. I secure my arms around the base of her ass once her face is in the vicinity with my dick.

"Undo me, Genesis."

She palms my dick through my jeans before she finally frees my cock. It juts to attention, ready to be sucked. My tongue licks a path between her opening and her ass. She tightens up, but I smile because I will be taking her here soon. For now, though, I have lined us up for a little sixty-nine. Without being told, she grabs my cock and takes me to the back of her throat. Feeling her suck my dick upside down gives me pause.

"*Hmmm*," she hums around my dick, and the sensation is un-fucking-believable.

I thrust my hardened length into her mouth and time it with the thrusts of my tongue inside her pussy. My nose is buried between her ass cheeks as I work to go deeper with every thrust. The smell of her combined with the slow attention she gives my cock have my legs stiffening. I'm getting close. She plays with my balls while licking the vein that runs underneath the head of my dick. It jumps with each pass of her tongue. She goes back to sucking me, taking me deeper each time until she has my entire dick in her mouth. *Holy shit*. I can feel the tingle begin to creep up my balls in this position.

I need her to slow down because it's getting increasingly hard not to explode in her mouth. I slap her ass once more, and she's startled for a second. A second is all I need. Once her mouth is away from my cock, I flip her upright once more. Her petite body is easy to switch things up. This time her legs are around my waist. I allow her to slide down my body until that wet pussy of hers is sitting just above my cock. No priming needed. I slam into her, and I have to hold on to her tightly. She arches her back and instantly begins to ride my dick. All shyness forgotten. I don't move at first. I let her set the rhythm—do what feels good to her—then I slowly join the pace she has set for us. The sound of her soaking pussy echoes over the music that is still playing and the running shower as my balls slap against her ass.

Genesis

I'm so lost in Elysian right now. Madison's little intrusion is long forgotten. This fucking sex god wants me. *Only me.* My pussy feels so full as I grip his every thrust. I need him deeper still, but the grip he has on my hips is restricting my movements. He's only giving me the amount of dick he wants me to have.

"Please go deeper," I beg, and he arches an eyebrow at me. He angles his hips and slams into me a few times, and my pussy become an inferno. He slows his pace, but I need hard, deep, and fast.

"Can't come yet, baby," he teases as he slides his dick out of me. My pussy immediately clenches at its disappearance.

He stands me back on my feet, and my legs feel weak. Holy hell, this man is strong. His lifts and then flips have my head swimming. I need a second to adjust to the position change. I didn't even know he had that in him, but it's hot as hell. He walks us over to my bed. I don't know where Loren is, and I can't be bothered to care.

"Get out of your head and get your sexy ass on the bed, love," he commands. I wobble over to the bed and crawl onto it. "I like that view. Stay just like that." I'm on all fours for him. He walks up behind me and slaps each ass cheek again. The delicious sting has my pussy dripping with need. I clench my pussy to dull the ache, but it only intensifies. "So fucking wet," he says.

"Fuck me, Elysian. I need your thick cock to fill me. Make me come."

"Don't forget that you asked for it," he warns as he kneels to lick me from behind again. The feeling is fucking amazing, but then he stops. His teasing has me so wound up; I feel like I'm about to explode. He builds me up over and over again, only to forbid me from having my release. I don't know how much more I can take. "Head down and ass up, baby, so that pussy opens up for me."

Fuck, I love his dirty talk. He can have anything he wants if he will just let me come. I do as he instructs, and he inserts a few fingers. He massages my insides before replacing his fingers with the tip of his beautiful cock. I throb around him. I back my ass up to him until his cock is resting at the hilt. He restricts me from moving farther, so I can feel his girth. I put a greater arch in my back to entice him to move. I need him to come undone. He wraps my hair in his fist and pulls at the same time he slams into me. I meet him stroke for stroke, my legs beginning to feel weak as my orgasm nears. Sensing that I'm close, he grabs me by the waist and flips me onto my back.

"Now I'm going to give you all the cock that you've been waiting for." He pushes my legs over his shoulders and eases into me. In this position, his cock is almost too much. He starts slowly, but then he finally comes undone. He fucks me hard and fast as he deepens his strokes. "Fuuuuuck, baby," he screams as he pulls out and comes all over my stomach. I close my eyes because the out-of-body experience is so foreign. I couldn't move even if I wanted to. Multiple orgasms roll into one, paralyzing me to the spot.

"Gah. You've wrecked me," I admit. "But in a good way."

"Feel better?" he questions.

"Much."

"Good. You may want to do something about that shower that's still running. Once you can move again, that is."

"Are you leaving?"

"I'm afraid so, my little sex kitten. I have work from Penn State that I need to catch up on. Plus, I don't want Loren to have to sleep in someone else's room again tonight. It's not fair to her."

"You're right. And I have work I need to catch up on too. Glad you came by for a fuck-by at least."

"A fuck-by?" His eyebrows knit in confusion.

"You know ... like a drive-by, but with your cock." I giggle.

"You dirty girl. I must say the potty mouth becomes you," he teases. "Night, love."

He goes into the bathroom to turn the shower off before he leaves. I miss his fullness already. I force myself to get out of bed and take that shower that's been on hold for his sneak fuck attack. Of course there is no more hot water, so a cold shower it is. Nothing can erase this silly grin I'm wearing. I know I need to lighten up and ignore Madison. She wants him, but I've had him. And plan to have him over and over again, so she can take a fucking hike. I don't know what this is between us, but I don't need a label. All I need are the orgasms he gives me. "Bloodstream" continues to play on repeat, but it definitely takes on a whole new meaning. Elysian is in more than my bloodstream, and I'm no longer denying it.

CHAPTER EIGHTEEN

Genesis

I startled out of my sleep in a drenching sweat. My bed is soaked, and my body is on fire. I can feel the heat underneath my skin. "Loren," I choke out.

I don't know what's happening to me. I stumble out my bed into the pitch blackness. "Loren," I call out again, hoarsely. I'm halfway to her bed when she pops up out of her sleep.

"Holy shit! What's going on?"

She chants a string of words I've never heard her use before, but the lights flicker on.

"I can't breathe," I flail, grasping at my neck. "It feels like someone is choking me." Panic begins to set in.

Loren rushes to me and sits me on her bed. "You're soaking wet. I should get my uncle. Your body is burning up with fever. I thought your body temp was lower than the average human."

"It is," I agree between pants for breath. "Elysian is the hot one. *Elysian!*"

"Elysian, What?" she asks as I jump from her bed.

"We're connected, remember? I'm not the one being choked ... he is. I'm experiencing his stress-induced heat." I manage to get out the words before I bolt from the room and into the night. The air is crisp around me but does little to cool me down.

Suddenly, I dash—an ability I've never been able to bring forth until now. I watch as the buildings begin to blur around me, but somehow, I still know which direction to take to get to his dorm. As I get closer, the invisible hold around my neck loosens, and I can breathe easier. The doors of Wickman's Hall come upon me fast, and I haven't given much thought as to how I was going to stop. I brace myself for impact, but instead, I feel a steady vibration pass over me. I open my eyes that I hadn't realized I closed only to be surprised that I'm on the other side. I'm *inside* Elysian's freaking dorms. I don't have time to be amazed at all this shit I've been able to do, though. I need to find him. I know he's in room 1102, so he has to be on the first floor. I dash for a second time, and I find myself inside his room within seconds. He's alone other than his roommate in the bed on the opposite side of the room. Then I hear him cry out in the darkness. Only a sliver of light filters through the window, but it's enough. I go to him just as he tosses and turns, and his body is burning up.

"No," he yells suddenly.

I grab him, but he bucks me off with so much force that I fly into the air. My back hits the wall over the mini fridge after which point, I slide down the wall and knock down the dishes sitting on them.

"Ah ..." I scream out as excruciating pain wracks my body. Tears immediately stream down my face. I can't move. The pain is relentless, and now my head begins to throb.

"What the fuck?" Brody yells, startled, rushing to turn on the light. He's a shapeshifter—werewolf.

Now that we're bathed in light, Elysian sits up in his bed. Confusion blankets his features.

"Genesis?" I'm glad to see that he's okay, but words fail me. "Babe, what are you doing here?"

He dashes to my side faster than I can blink. The door swings open before I can speak. It's Mr. Blakey with Loren flanked at his side.

"Is everyone okay in here? Are we alone?" he asks. I have no idea how Loren was able to get him here so fast.

"Okay? Apparently not. I have no idea what the hell is going on," Brody reacts.

"Me either," Elysian seconds. "But Genesis is hurt."

Mr. Blakey takes in the scene of broken dishes and turned over mini fridge around me. He points at the body-sized dent in the drywall.

"What happened there?" he asks, now examining the dent.

"Me," I whisper between unrelenting pain. "I happened."

Elysian draws in a sharp breath as he realizes that I hit the wall before landing here. "How? And what are you doing in my room in the middle of the night?"

I try to speak again, but I can't form the words. Now that the adrenaline is beginning to wear off, the pain is becoming increasingly unbearable. More tears stream down my face.

Mr. Blakey runs a single hand down my body what I've come to know as his warlock assessment. "We need to get her to the infirmary now! We'll figure out what went wrong here later."

He lifts me into his arms effortlessly and heads out the door, leaving Elysian, Loren, and Brody to follow. We don't stop until he lays me down on a stretcher in the infirmary. He ominously pulls a curtain around us from overhead.

"Don't come any closer. You don't want to see this," he warns them on the other side of the curtain. Fear rivals the pain. What was he about to do to me that he didn't want them to witness? "Genesis, listen carefully. You have a severed spinal cord and broke your back at T1. Your spinal cord is unable to heal itself because of the compression against it from the fracture. I need reset it by further fracturing it in the opposite direction. Once the spinal cord is free, it will heal as well as the fractures."

"Will it hurt?" I ask, scared out my fucking mind.

"I'm afraid so. I could give you something for pain, but like the alcohol, it will slow down your ability to heal yourself."

"No," Elysian objects, pushing past the curtain.

"It's okay. I'll do whatever needs to be done. Just don't leave me, okay?"

Sadness reflect in his eyes as his shoulders drop. "I won't leave you."

He grabs my hand and squeezes. I nod to let Mr. Blakely know that I'm ready. He gives one last look over at Elysian before he comes to stand at my side. He contorts my body into a fetal position facing him, but I can't feel anything below my waist. I close my eyes, yet Elysian never lets go of my hand. Mr. Blakely centers his elbow in the middle of my back, and that's all I'm able to feel before pain, even more excruciating than before, rips through the top half of my body. I scream out in agony, and my eyes shoot open. Elysian visibly tenses, looking more broken than I feel.

"That's the worst of it," Mr. Blakely assures.

"Is she going to be okay?" Elysian asks. "I remember having the nightmare. Did I do this?"

"It's not your fault," I explain.

"Fuuuuuck!" he yells, letting go of my hand.

"Language, son," Mr. Blakely warns.

"I'm sorry. It's just hard to hear that I've done this to her for a second time."

"It wasn't on purpose, Elysian," I point out. "You were having a nightmare. When I grabbed for you … you reacted to whatever you were dreaming about. I should have just called out your name to wake you."

"No. You did nothing wrong. You are not to blame here. How did you even know I was having a nightmare?"

Loren and Brody pull back the curtain. "She woke up in a sweat with a sensation of being choked. She woke me up, and when I felt her, I could feel how hot she was. When I mentioned that it wasn't like her to be so hot, she realized that she was absorbing whatever you were experiencing. She thought someone was here in your dorm choking you."

All the color drains from his face. "So you came all the way here because you thought someone was harming me?" I nod my affirmation since the pain hasn't subsided. "And then I break you for your efforts." He shakes his head in disgust.

"So she was physically hot to the touch?" Mr. Blakely asks Loren.

"Yes," she confirms.

"Your connection to each other is growing," Mr. Blakely states. "It's no longer just sensations shared. You're affecting each other on a molecular level."

"I was able to dash here and go through the front door and the door to his room too," I confess as I grit my teeth through pain.

"She phased? That's phenomenal. Your powers are definitely growing at an exponential rate that we didn't calculate."

"What's phase?" Elysian inquires.

"Phasing is the ability to vibrate at the same frequency of an object in order to pass through it.

Genesis was able to phase through two locked doors. Dashing and phasing are two new powers that manifested for her tonight, not to mention her molecular energy absorbed yours to manifest your heat. It was a beacon to her to signal that you were in trouble," Mr. Blakely explains.

"But I wasn't in danger. It was just a nightmare," he rebuts.

"The threat was real enough to trigger your entangled response. What were you dreaming about?" Mr. Blakely asks.

"It's a little fuzzy now, but I was at the front of the school. I could see the fountain when suddenly one of the students started choking me. I couldn't escape his grip no matter how hard I wrestled him. Finally, I managed to come out on top. I was about to land a punch when he morphed into a wolf. I dashed, but I couldn't shake him. He was gaining on me, and he nearly had me until woke up. That must have been the moment that Genesis grabbed me. I thought it was him—I thought he had caught me. I'm so sorry, Genesis," Elysian apologizes again.

"It's okay," I assure him. "I can finally feel the pain starting to dissipate."

Mr. Blakely runs a hand along my body once again. "You're healing," he confirms. "This is neither of your faults. Something between you two has definitely evolved, and it's going to take more observation and caution as things progress even more. This a new phenomenon for us all since we've never had any half gods at our academy. You two are the learning curve."

"What happens now?" Loren asks.

"For now, Genesis will stay the night here to rest under observation. We will run labs in the morning to see if your baselines have changed," he says, looking back and forth between Elysian and I. "I don't know why you had a dream about a shapeshifter attack, but we'll dig more into it in the morning. You're both safe, and that's what matters."

"I'm not leaving her," Elysian insists as he pull a chair from the corner next to my stretcher.

"Didn't think you were, Mr. Remis. I'll let your professors know that you're excused from your classes tomorrow for a thorough workup." He turns to Loren and Brody. "The two of you are not excused, so get back to your dorms," he says to Loren and Brody. "Thank you for calling me, Loren."

He gives us a wave as we watch his retreating back. I have no doubt he is sending another staff member in to observe me for the night. Loren kisses her hand and presses it against my cheek.

"You've had a rough night, babe, but I know you're in good hands. We'll talk tomorrow when you're back to yourself, and I can squeeze you. Come on, Brody. Let's let them be."

"See you tomorrow, and we'll talk," I agree.

She and Brody leave together, but Elysian pulls his chair closer to my bedside.

"You can't sleep in that chair," I tell him. "Why don't you go to your room and get some rest, and I'll see you in the morning."

"Not a chance, babe. I couldn't possibly sleep with you here like this. What does this all mean? What if we are in danger? What if I had been attacked? You have to promise that if you get that overwhelming feeling again that you won't come to my aid—that you won't try to save me."

"Not a chance, babe," I retort.

"And that's what I'm afraid of. I would never be able to forgive myself if something happened to you again because of me. Seeing you like this is killing me, already. Why do you have to be so stubborn?"

"So if you sensed I was in danger, does that mean you would ignore the sensation?"

"Of course not," he answers, incredulously.

"Ditto," I shoot back. He lets out an exasperated breath. "I have your back the same way you have mine. We're entangled for a reason, so you're stuck with me."

He rubs the back of my hand but finally acquiesces. He puts his head down on the rail of the stretcher, and I close my eyes. I hear when someone joins us for a night of observation duty, but neither of us gives them an acknowledgment. As the pain fades, I succumb to the blackness behind my eyelids. I can sleep now knowing that the man slowly taking possession of my heart is safe.

CHAPTER NINETEEN

Elysian

Walking across the courtyard, I shield my eyes to filter out some of the morning light. I left Genesis sound asleep back at the infirmary since we only have a couple more hours before we meet with Mr. Blakey and Professor Winters to discuss last night's ordeal. As I approach the fountain, it gives me pause. This is where all the chaos unfolded in my dream. The hairs on my arm prickle, and a lump forms in my throat. An ominous feeling creeps over me, and my feet become lead. I take in my surroundings, immediately becoming on guard. Nothing. I blow out a breath of ease in reprieve, but it's short-lived. I feel him before my eyes ever lay eyes on him. Our gaze locks. Tall, blonde, and ordinary. This guy doesn't look like a physical threat; however, I'm not fooled. This isn't my first time to see him. I remember very vividly how our interaction progressed. His affect and clothes are identical to our last meeting. This can't be simply a coincidence. His eyes never leave mine—as if he's calculating his next move.

Do I let him make that move or do I go on the offense? Students pass by, unaware of the danger in their midst. Time is ticking, the opportunity for the element of surprise running out.

"Can I help you?" the blonde guys ask, challengingly. "Why are you just staring at me?"

"Just trying to get by, man. You stopped first, so I followed suit."

"Well, you were in my way. I'm waiting for you to move."

I look him up and down. I could easily bench press this kid, but if my dream last night was indeed a foreshadow, I know that his appearance is a disguise. I need to get back to Genesis, so if giving this dipshit a pass is what it takes, then I will step aside. I take two steps to the left, intent on avoiding engagement, but it's futile. This ordinary asshat clotheslines me before I make a third step, and now, I'm lying with my back on the ground.

"Too late. I'm sorry, but you don't get a second chance. Word around campus is that you're a demigod. I think you need a little introduction to your place here. There's only room for one alpha here."

"What the ...?"

I attempt to get up and unleash the powers I've learned to access on this moron. I've seen the future, so I know my wrestling moves won't be enough. He's quick, though. He descends upon me within seconds, still in his human form. I tap into the strength that I possess and use both hands to shove at the center of his chest. He flies, transitioning midair. I dash before his wolf form can touch the ground. He never stood a chance to catch me. Vampires are faster than wolves, and I'm even faster. I dash into the infirmary, grab Genesis with one swipe, and continue my speed to Mr. Blakely's office. He startles at the intrusion. He and Professor Winters are already in discussion.

"Elysian?" Mr. Blakey asks, confused. We have another hour before we were supposed to meet.

"It wasn't a dream," I rush out as I set Genesis on her feet. "It was a precognition."

"Slow down, son. Tell me exactly what happened since I saw the two of you last night."

I start from the beginning. I tell him about the incident in the courtyard by the fountain—how the guy was exactly how I remember him from the dream. I describe in detail what this douchebag looks like. I had the advantage because I knew he would shapeshift into a wolf, so I was able to avoid the physical assault that I knew was coming.

"Oh, dear. We need to review the campus footage to see who this student is," Professor Winters says.

"That's not all. He said that everyone knew that I was a demigod, and that I needed a lesson on my place because there is only room for one alpha."

"I'll send for Jason. He is the known alpha of the wolves here. His appearance isn't as you've described, but

I bet he'll knows who we're looking for," Mr. Blakely ponders. He wastes no time making a call.

"How are you feeling today, Genesis?" Professor Winters asks. With how fast everything happened, I didn't even take a second to assess that she was healed. She walks over to window to pull the curtain back, so I guess we have our answer.

"Physically, I'm fine. Nothing hurts. It's still miraculous that I can heal myself this quickly." She peers out the window, on edge. I can sense her tension. "Mentally, I'm alarmed and unprepared. The word is out on what we are. How many other students are going to come for us? Are we safe here?"

"I can assure you that you are. We will get to the bottom of this ... today! This academy is a haven for our students while they learn to control their abilities. There is zero tolerance for those who pose any threat or compromise our mission," Mr. Blakely snaps. "Jason is on the way."

"Our powers are growing, but I'd feel a lot better if I knew how to readily access them. Last night I was able to phase and dash, but I have no clue how to do it again. How can I feel confident that I can protect myself ... protect us, if I can't unleash my powers at will?"

Genesis walks back over to us. Her weariness hangs heavily on my shoulders. I wish I could ease her fears. Neither of us asked for this.

"I will do whatever it takes to protect you," I promise.

"And that's precisely my point," Mr. Blakely interrupts. "You shouldn't feel the need for protection here. The threat is outside."

"You sent for me, Mr. Blakey?" A lean but muscular dude enters. His coal black hair is the opposite of blonde. He looks nothing like the guy from the courtyard.

He surveys the room and takes us all in, his stance on guard. Mr. Blakely explains what just happened by the fountain without revealing my class or that the attack was my premonition. He describes the guy with the details that I provided. "Do you know who this guy is?" Mr. Blakely questions.

"I think you're talking about Daniel. He doesn't go here, but I've seen him on campus not too long ago. He's Mitchell's cousin."

"How is that even possible? None of the faculty have granted approval for him as a visitor. Looks like I need to summon Mitchell. He knows the rules."

"I'll do that now," Professor Winters volunteers.

"I'm not one to rat out any part of my pack, but I don't owe any allegiance to that guy. He and Mitchell have been challenging my position at every turn."

"So you're telling me that this isn't Daniel's first time here on campus—unauthorized?"

"Unfortunately not, sir. I know I should have come forward sooner, so I apologize for my part in this mess. The word is spreading rapidly around campus that we have half gods in our midst, and some may feel threatened. I don't."

"Well, I have a few words to spread around campus of

my own. Anyone causing a disturbance will be expelled permanently. Zero tolerance and no second chances." He turns to Genesis and me. "This breach was with the aid of another student. Measures will be taken so that there isn't another," Mr. Blakely assures us.

"The two of you will come with me to the lab so I can give you a physical. We will discuss the new powers you've both tapped into since practicing in class," Professor Winters informs.

Genesis and I reluctantly follow her out of Mr. Blakely's office, leaving him alone with Jason. I wanted a chance to identify this guy—to see firsthand that he is apprehended. He's not a student here, so what punishment could they possible enforce? What would they do to the cousin? What are these measures they plan to implement to assure our safety? I have so many questions, but I will put my trust in the faculty. Genesis needs someone she can lean on, so I will be optimistic for her. We're safe here.

I dash, lift ridiculous amount of weight, and unleash fire balls into a plexiglass enclosed box. It has a higher heat resistant of 360 degrees Fahrenheit, but I'm still able to melt it. These powers are all performed under the direction of Professor Winters and Professor Guenther. I look on as Genesis, surprisingly but successfully, accesses her newfound powers. She dashes, creates bigger ice sculptures, and phases through the portable wooden door brought in for this exercise. Her faces lights up with disbelief as she squeals around the room.

"I did it," she yells repeatedly. "I just focused on what I wanted to do, and poof, I made it happen!"

Professor Winters and Professor Guenther look at each other, but I can't read if it's intrigue or worry. "I have a personal question to ask of you two," Professor Winters begins. "Normally, I wouldn't, but I promise it's relevant."

"Okay," Genesis answers, looking over at me. "What is it?"

"Obviously, you two are unlike anyone we've had at this academy, so your abilities and the rate at which they have developed have been an ongoing lesson for all of us," she continues. "But I've been researching half gods since your arrival and called on the aid of some very powerful witches. Not all half gods are entangled. Apparently, if they are, it's purposely so."

"What do you mean purposeful, and what question do you have for us?" I prod.

"I'm getting to that," she assures. "It means that your divinity was strategically mated for a purpose. You were never meant to be just half gods. You see, entangled gods are even more powerful that the average demigod or demigoddess. Your powers have the ability to be greater than a second-generation god or below. That means no half god will be comparable to your capabilities. You're even stronger together—entangled."

"So we make each other stronger?" I clarify.

"Not just that. We were only partially right about you two. You were connected before, but from the looks of your exponentially developed powers, you're now entangled."

"What's the difference?" Genesis asks.

"Before when you were connected, you subconsciously sought each other out and could absorb some of each other's energy like pain. Once you connect on a mate level, your powers evolve quickly as well as your ability to absorb and sense each other's energy on a greater scale," Professor Guenther explains.

"Connect on a mate level?" I think I know what he means, but I need to be sure.

"Mate as in sexually active. And therein lies the question. Have the two of you mated or, shall I say, had sexual intercourse?" Professor Winters asks. Genesis flushes crimson. Was the professor really asking if we've fucked? "That's exactly what I'm asking ... just a little less graphic," she confirms.

How can I ever forget that they all have this mind reading ability? "Well then, yes," I answer when it's obvious that Genesis is too embarrassed to reply.

"There's no shame, dear," Professor Winters tells Genesis. I wonder what her thoughts revealed that's so shameful. "You're both adults. You're not being chastised. We're just trying to explain how this changes things."

"Yeah. Like what is our true purpose. Why were we bred to be stronger than second-generation gods? Does

QUANTUM ENTANGLEMENT: PART ONE

that mean our parents are first generation like Zeus or Poseidon?"

"I don't think so. The offspring of those powerful gods are well documented in our history. Our best guess is that you are the children of second-generation gods, bred for a purpose of entanglement. The why is unknown, but the important thing here is to know that you're both safe. The *why* will reveal itself eventually. We will just continue to monitor your development and help you harness and control your powers as they unfold," Professor Winters says.

"So you're saying that mating between us was inevitable?" Genesis speaks up, blushing once again. Her replacement of fucking with the word mating is too adorable. I love that I know how to get her shyness to take a hike.

"I can still read your thoughts, Mr. Remis," Professor Winters reminds. "I think the two of you have had enough excitement for today. Take the rest of the day off. Professor Thorne will be expecting you both in class early tomorrow, though." He nods in confirmation.

Between last night and today, excitement is an understatement. I can sense Genesis's apprehension lingering. We have the rest of today free, so I'm making it my mission to ease her worries. We can worry about our purpose on another day. The most important thing is that we're safe. I believe that, and I want to make sure that she does too.

CHAPTER TWENTY

Genesis

E lysian arrives to pick me up for our afternoon outing. I've been on edge since this morning—waiting for the next attack. Mr. Blakey and Professor Winters have both assured us that the breach will be dealt with swiftly and measures have been put in place to ensure increased security. These so-called measures were purposely vague. Elysian thought we could use a little normalcy—a distraction from the surprise attack that plays on a loop. We're nearly out the door when he glances down at my feet.

"Those goddess sandals are quite fitting in the literal sense, but they're not suitable for the day I have planned. I would advise tennis shoes." He kisses the tip of my nose, turns me around, and swats my ass to steer me back into the room. I expect him to follow, but he doesn't. I throw on my pink Converse and put my hair in a top knot before retuning back to the doorway. Elysian grabs the elastic band that is securing my untamable hair in place.

"I didn't mean change the hair. I love it wild and untamed. The red waves are sexy, and it's a constant turn-on." He runs his hands through my hair for emphasis as he kisses me passionately. "Let's get out of here before I change my mind."

"I wouldn't object." I run my hand up and down his impeccable chest.

"Who is this insatiable sex kitten that has taken over?" he chides.

I roll my eyes in mock exasperation. He knows he likes my growing sexual appetite. I don't call him out on it, though, or else we may not make it from this room. I see his unattended motorcycle waiting at the curb. He gets on first, passes me a helmet, and then leans the bike over just enough for me to get on.

"Where are we going?" I inquire.

"I thought we'd head down to the creek again today." He grabs my hand and rubs tiny circles over my skin. He must sense my doubt. Madison always seems to pop up out of nowhere when we're together, and the creek is one of her favorite places to unwind. "We'll take in some of nature's beauty and get some fresh air away from the dorms. Don't worry, we'll go to a different area of the creek."

We spend the day hiking along the creek. He was right. If the thick brush is any indication, there isn't much foot traffic on this side of the creek. Lush green trees stretch beyond our sight, surrounding us. Elysian and I walk hand in hand, taking in the sights and listening to nature's sounds. It's nice to be able to completely let down our guard without fear of being in more danger. The day feels suspiciously like a date with a boyfriend, but I won't mention it at the risk of him ending it. He hasn't initiated any labels for us, and we don't need one. This morning has been absolutely perfect. Around lunchtime, he surprises me with a picnic set up for us near the water.

We're completely alone. He has managed to secure a spot well removed from the campus, offering privacy while still being on the campus grounds. I look at him, and he's smiling at me. He doesn't realize this romantic moment only blurs the lines further of us just being friends. These glimpses into his caring side make me want more even though I would never push for it. I love that I can be so carefree around him—be the nerdy girl who everyone else overlooks. But not him. He sees me, and I see him. He's more than the insanely gorgeous jock know-it-all that I first took him for. *So much more.* As he unpacks the backpack, same as last time, I swear I gain five pounds just looking at the delicious spread. There's hummus, crackers, chocolate-covered strawberries, various cheeses, a fruit salad, and a pinot noir. Every food thought out in detail for a vegetarian.

"This all looks amazing. When did you have time to coordinate all this?"

His dimpled chin is addicting. "I have my ways, but I'll never tell. This is me bringing the swoon."

"And swoon-worthy it is. Thank you for doing all of this for me. You sure know how to make a girl feel special." I give him a soft peck on the cheek. He uses this opportunity to lay my head across his lap. He feeds me a chocolate strawberry, and I'm in heaven.

"The strawberries go really well with the wine," he says.

I attempt to sit up to grab a plastic wine glass, but he pushes me back down on his legs. I'm facing him so he can see me pout. "How am I supposed to try the wine with my strawberries if I'm lying on my back?"

"Like this," he says. He takes a sip after pouring himself a glass, and I'm confused until he leans down and captures my lips with his. He transfers the wine from his mouth to mine, and it has to be the hottest thing I've ever experienced. *Holy hell.* Just as he did with the whiskey. It was erotic then, and it's erotic now. My breath hitches, and my chest heaves as I try to remember to breathe. This man is trying to kill me. "You like the wine, babe?"

I'm speechless, so I simply nod. He takes another sip of his wine and repeats the same erotic offering. I refuse to let his mouth go this time. I deepen the kiss, and he groans. I feel his hardness penetrating my back. "Don't start something in public that you aren't prepared to finish because I'll fuck you right here on this picnic blanket," he threatens. His lustful cerulean blue eyes pierce mine, and I know he's not bluffing. "It's so easy to lose control with you."

"The feeling is mutual." I'd never been this open and

vulnerable with any man. He makes me feel sexy and desired. He continues to feed me strawberries, and I must say that I love the pampering.

I rise on my knees so I can feed him too. When I straddle his thighs, he growls.

"Must I remind you that we're in a public place?"

"Umm hmm," I reply teasingly. I know exactly what I'm doing to him. If I didn't, his hard-on poking me through my jean shorts would be a dead giveaway. He grips my hips to grind me down farther onto me.

"Behave, my little spitfire." We finish our picnic with me on his lap, but he doesn't seem to mind. "I have one more surprise."

"What is it?" I squirm in his lap like an excited toddler.

"Come. It wouldn't be a surprise if I told you." He grabs my hand, and we trek back to where he parked his bike and find a two-person kayak waiting there. That definitely wasn't sitting there before. I gawk at him in shock. He reaches for the life jackets and passes me one to prepare for a little sunset kayaking. The romance factor has just exploded off the charts.

"I don't know what to say. Today has been an adventure. I haven't had this much fun in a long time. But how? This kayak wasn't here when you parked your bike."

"You deserve it. Normally, I wouldn't reveal my sources, but I'm in a nostalgic mood. The kayak belongs to my roommate, Brody. When I found out that he owned this little gem, I knew I had to plan a special day around it. I told him when to drop it off, so the surprise wouldn't be ruined."

He takes a seat in the back of the kayak and guides me to the front. The sun has now set, and the lights of the cityscape set the ambiance. I can't see Elysian, but I can feel his energy.

His purposeful stroke of the paddle compensates for my beginner's efforts. I revel in this memory-making moment. I turn slightly and see he's staring at me intently. I mouth, "Thank you," and he smiles. By the time our sunset rendezvous ends, I'm hungry and not for food. When we make it back to my dorm, we head straight to the bathroom. No detours. We are both ready to release this sexual tension that has been building all day.

"Let me draw us a bath," he suggests. Oooh, this is new. I couldn't be more thankful that Loren is not here.

"Okay."

I'm not going to argue with that. Elysian lights the rose-scented candles and pours bath oils as the water runs. He makes quick work of ridding himself of his clothes before peeling off mine. I watch his dick rise to the occasion as he removes my last stitch of clothing. He gets into the tub first and watches as I get in position in front of him.

"Lie back. Let me see you."

I lie with my back against his chest as he uses a pouf sponge to wet my breasts. He plants small kisses on the side of my face, and I feel myself melting into him. He uses the sponge to caress every inch of my body, which is on fire now, and I begin to squirm.

"Something wrong?"

He knows exactly what's wrong. I decide to give him a taste of his own medicine, so I turn to face him and straddle his lower legs, stretching the full length of the tub. I waste no time taking him in my hands and beginning a torturous stroke. A bead of liquid forms at the tip of his cock as it rises above the water line. He lets out a soft gasp. I lower my head closer to his bobbing cock, his legs stiffen in anticipation while the heat in his eyes sears me on the spot. I take my time licking the head before allowing my tongue to explore the underside of his shaft. His hands are tangled in my hair now, trying to guide my movements. I cup his sack as I hollow my cheeks and take him deep. My head bobs up and down on his length as though he's my favorite thing in the world, and it is. I love how I'm making him lose control.

"Shit. Please don't stop. Your mouth is fucking unbelievable." His appraisal makes me double my efforts. I want him to come completely undone. I'm so wet from seeing how turned on I'm making him. His legs stiffen once more, and I know he's close. "Baby, I'm going to come. You need to stop if you don't want me to explode in your mouth."

I'm thrilled that he's completely at my mercy. I answer his warning with harder suction and increase my stroking. He should have known how this was going to play out. He surrenders his orgasm to me, and it's so thick I almost choke. I swallow every bit he has given me and lick my lips in satisfaction.

"Bath time is over," he growls. He is out of the tub in the blink of an eye. After he grabs me, he does a rush job of toweling us both dry, then turns me toward the room and slaps my ass. The stinging sensation causes moisture to build even more between my legs. "Get on the bed and spread your legs."

I comply without hesitation. He stealthily crawls between my legs and plants sensuous kisses along my inner thighs. My hips buck on their own accord but are held still in his masculine grasp. "Hold still, sweetheart."

"Elysian, please."

I'm already so wet and turned on from giving him head in the bath. My skin is alive with sensual overload, and I'm dying for him to be inside me. His teasing is driving me insane. I almost come undone at the first lick of his skilled tongue. He sucks on my nub while he slips one, then two fingers inside me. He crooks his finger in a "*come here*" motion, and I scream out in pure ecstasy.

"Fuck, yes. Your pussy is gripping the hell out of my finger." He continues his feast until another orgasm rolls on top of the first one. I grip his shoulder-length hair as I ride his face. My knees quiver around his head before they fall limp in exhaustion. He crawls up the length of my body and kisses me with fervor. He places his tip at my entrance, sliding in with ease. I moan with pleasure as he thrusts his hips in a delicious, steady tempo. He begins to suck on my neck, and I writhe in his arms. I love how his weight and masculine build encase me in his warmth.

I can no longer lie to myself. I'm head over heels in love with this man. He angles his hips, and this new position has us both splintering into pieces. I feel him throbbing inside me.

"Damn, Genesis. You feel so good."

He places tiny kisses along my jawline and massages my breast. He flicks my nipple, and I feel a bite of pain. He leans down and takes one into his mouth and begins to suck. I can feel the moisture pooling between my folds again. He alternates nibbling and sucking both breasts, and now I am on fire. I feel his erection lengthening along my thigh right before he enters me again. Three orgasms later, I'm sated and bone tired. He disappears to get us a washcloth. When he comes back, he cleans me up, and all I can do is lie here during this intimate moment.

"Are you worn out?"

He gives me that wicked grin that I love and winks. If I weren't so tired, I would beg him to take me again.

"Yes, babe. You wore me out," I admit. He climbs into bed with me, and I smile. "I love sleeping with you." I flush crimson after realizing I just admitted this out loud. I don't want to spook him. I cover my eyes with my hands, afraid to read his expression. He removes my hands and places a kiss on the tip of my nose.

"No regrets, love. Always speak freely. I actually like sleeping with you, too." He pulls me closer and brings the covers over us. "I don't know how long before Loren comes back, but I can't make myself leave tonight. I want to be with you just like this. In a bubble that's just us."

"I like this whole bubble idea. Nothing can touch us inside our bubble. It's just us inside with great sex." I chortle.

He squeezes me and bites my shoulder. My back is to his front. "Great sex, huh? I would say fucktastic, but great works too. We need an abundance of it here in our bubble, only coming out for food."

I am speechless. Maybe, just maybe he's falling for me too. I don't want to read too much into it. I can't set myself up for that type of fall if this is just fun for him. If his tenderness is any indication, I would say that's not the case, but I can't be one hundred percent certain. It's not like he asked me to be his girl or anything. I won't push him, but I'm happy with our progress. I snuggle into him and let myself fall into a deep, peaceful sleep.

CHAPTER TWENTY-ONE

Elysian

I wrap the white bath towel around my waist after stepping out of the shower. I was tempted to let Genesis join me, but that would have only resulted in us both being late to class. Thankfully, we only have Managing Expectations with Professor Thorne. Rules, rules, and more rules. I walk into the bedroom just as Madison enters. And she is not alone. Loren flanks her with a knowing grin on her face. I know she came back last night because I heard her awful attempt at trying to be quiet. She was gone when I got up so that played into my decision to shower here. I don't have a private bath in my dorm. I didn't want to risk having to wait for an available shower, and I couldn't attend class with dried jizz from last night's activities.

"What in the tea do we have here?" Madison asks, her eyes traveling south to my semi-hard cock pressed against the cotton.

"Meet our third roommate," Loren jokes. "I dig it," she adds, letting her own eyes take in the bulge behind the towel.

"I didn't realize you were back," I apologize to Loren. "Or that you had company."

"Oh, I'm just company now." I was going ask what she thought she was before, but she continues with the reason for her visit. "Whatever. I just came by to see if Genesis and Loren were coming out tonight. I had no idea you'd be here."

Her eyes evade me. Her voice thick with hurt. She doesn't know about the incident from yesterday. How could we still go out?

"Sure. I'm down," I hear Genesis respond. "I need to see my parents."

"Maybe we should sit this weekend out," Loren proposes, on the same page with me.

"On the contrary," Madison challenges. "Something is up with the wolf pack. Nobody is saying what, but I know they've gotten into some trouble. James is being tight-lipped, but I know he can't make it out with us. While the faculty is distracted with the pack, it's easier for us to leave."

James is one of the wolves we met at the campfire. He didn't come out with us the first time we left the campus. I look over at Genesis who has her arms crossed over her chest. "I need to see them," she mouths.

"Fine, but Genesis and I both have people we want to meet up with. How will that work?"

"We leave the same way as last time. We'll exchange numbers, but we will all meet up at the same diner at two a.m. This way we can all ride back together."

"Sounds easy enough," I admit.

I don't really have anyone to meet up with because of the short notice, but I can still call my folks and reach out to my buddy Josh. I'll leave some room in my planning in case Genesis wants me to go with her to see her parents.

"See you guys tonight, then."

She leaves, and I feel somewhat sorry for her. I didn't plan on her seeing me this way in Genesis's room. However, now it reinforces that nothing between us will ever happen.

"That towel really suites you." Loren snickers, interrupting my thoughts. "But in all seriousness, are you two really going to go out tonight after everything that's happened in the last couple of days?"

"I'm trying to stay positive," Genesis remarks. "That was an isolated incident with a jealous, power-hungry prick. It was at least clear that he was working with his dumb cousin without the support of the pack here. I don't know what the outcome is, but we can't live our days in fear."

"I guess she has a point," I agree. "We have to trust that the faculty has it handled. The best way to get over it is to resume our lives before all this mess came about."

After kissing Genesis on the forehead, I grab my clothes off her floor and take them to change in the bathroom. I know that everything I just said is optimistic. I just hope I'm not wrong. Something still isn't right, yet I can't pinpoint what it is.

I wake up in drenched sweat and disoriented. It takes a few looks around my dorm to realize I'm in my room safe. It was just a dream. *Fuck*. No, it wasn't. It was another precognition, and I need to get to Genesis ASAP. We can't go out tonight. None of us can. I glance at my phone. It's nearly seven. I laid down for nap after class and have been sleep for a couple of hours. I can't waste any more time. I have to stop the plan to leave tonight. I grab my keys off the dresser and dash toward Genesis's room.

She's startled when I enter. It's only now that I just phased for the first time through the lock door. She sits up in her bed and rubs her eyes. Apparently, she'd laid down for a nap of her own. Loren walks out of the bathroom, obviously already dressed for tonight.

"Who let you in?" Loren asks, suspiciously.

"Nobody. I phased through the front entrance and your door."

"Shut up. You can phase too?" Genesis squeals.

"Apparently," I confirm.

"Yeah, except new powers usually mean a sign of trouble," Loren points out. "What have you come to say that required phasing?"

"Well, since you mentioned it, there is a reason I

rushed here. We can't go out tonight. I had another premonition."

"What?" Genesis hops off her bed and begin to pace. "What was it?"

"Danger is coming. I couldn't count them all, but a pack of wolves will breach the campus at first light when the veil comes down. I recognized Daniel's wolf form from his attack. This time, he's bringing reinforcements."

"Do you think it's possible that it was just a dream?" Loren asks. Her brows crinkle in worry.

"Even if it was, that's not a chance we can take," Genesis answers.

"Genesis is right. We have to assume my vision was accurate. And if that's the case, the attack will happen at the same moment we would be returning. We can't let them drop that cloak, and if the group leaves anyway without us, they will be stuck on the other side without their powers."

"I forgot about that. Our powers are bound to the jewelry we use for the reverse locator spell. We'd be defenseless on the other side and unable to warn or help the people here," Genesis points out.

"So what do we tell the group?" Loren asks. "I'm sure everyone is getting ready as we speak. They're not going to want cancel without some explanation."

"So we give them one," I suggest. "The truth."

"The truth?" Genesis mouth gasps in shock.

"Why not? I told you what Daniel said. It's spreading like wildfire around campus about what we are. Soon the attempted attack on me will too. If my precognition is true, we can't leave them in the dark."

The girls nod in agreement. Loren calls Madison and asks to have everyone meet up at the creek. We have the advantage for now, and we need a plan. Within thirty minutes, we've all arrived at the place we had our last hangout.

Madison is the last to arrive. She looks past me as she marches right up to Loren.

"Okay, someone tell me what's going on. What's the purpose of this little impromptu meetup?"

"You mentioned that something happened with the wolf pack this morning, and I can shed some light on that," I begin. This gets her attention. Her eyes narrow as she places a hand on her exposed hip.

"Okay. Tell us. And what does that have to do with us going out tonight?"

I start from the beginning—telling about my crazy nightmare and how the next day it came to fruition. I was only able to escape the attack because of the advance details from my dream. A collective gasp is heard around our circle, and this is before I tell them about today's precognition.

"Oh my God, Elysian. I'm so sorry. I had no idea what the two of you were going through," Madison apologizes, her tone softened. "I know I've been such a bitch."

"It's fine," I assure. "But there's more. I had another premonition a couple of hours ago. And this is even worse."

The widened eyes and silence from the group urge me to continue. I tell them about the pack that's coming—so many that I couldn't even count them all.

"But they're coming for you two, right?" Kristin asks.

"I was the target for the first attack, but the alpha here gave up Daniel's identity as well as his cousin's role in helping him breach this campus. My best guess is that I'm no longer his only target. Revenge is the motivation, and we don't know if it's with the academy as a whole or just Genesis and me along with the pack. Our best defense is to ensure they never breach the campus."

"I agree," Madison says. "We can't be on the other side of the gates when the fight comes to us. We have to be ready to fight!"

"If we get my uncle and the other faculty on this, we won't have to fight at all," Loren adds.

"The cloak is only down for five minutes at a time. How is that even enough time to get here? Wolves are fast, but not that fast. They can't dash or teleport," Matt points out.

"Because they just said that Mitchell's cousin has been on our campus. He could have mapped out landmarks to return to. They'd be waiting at the border for the drop of the cloak and won't need minutes to infiltrate," Madison explains.

"Why is it that we need a reverse locator spell on a piece of jewelry to find our way back here? Couldn't we have just used landmarks too?" Genesis prods.

"We could, but it's not as effective. The faculty are not

dumb. They routinely comb for landmarks that someone may have carved out and get rid of them. Plus, the jewelry also binds our power so we don't accidentally use them in public. It's our safety net and insurance that we won't lose our way back," Madison explains.

Loren is the first to stand from our circle. "I'm going to warn my uncle. Genesis and Elysian should come with me. The rest of us can meet back here in a couple of hours to see how we're going to proceed. But going out tonight is definitely out."

We all agree before Genesis and I follow Loren to Mr. Blakely's office. "Do you think he'll still be in his office this late?" I ask.

"Oh, trust me. He'll be there. This is his weekend to manage operations, and he's a workaholic," she ensures.

And she's correct. He looks a bit surprised to see us, and he's not alone. Professor Winters is with him. He ushers us inside, guessing that something is wrong.

"I would ask to what do I owe the pleasure, but I'm guessing at this hour, this is not a simple visit," Mr. Blakey says, gesturing for us to take a seat.

"Elysian had another precognition today, and since his first one came true, we knew we needed to warn you right away," Loren begins.

"What was it this time, dear?" Professor Winters ask, unable to hide the alarm in her voice.

"It's that Daniel guy again. But this time, he's bringing reinforcements. Lots of reinforcement. They're planning to strike at first light."

I'm careful not to mention that the attack will happen once the cloak comes down because we're not supposed to know about the scheduled drops.

"Daniel and Mitchell were both escorted off the campus today. There isn't a way to find their way back here. I'll personally cast a spell to sweep any residual landmarks leading back here just for added measure."

There he goes with the measures thing again. I was hoping that he'd be the one to mention the cloak and to ensure that they won't drop it.

"There were so many of them. What if they know of a way that you hadn't thought of? What if they've already used landmarks to arrive here and are now just waiting to first light?" I hint. "Then your spell to sweep the forest won't work."

"Listen, son. I know you're all worried, and your concerns are legitimate. But when I sweep the boundaries and forest, it will be for warmth as well. Wolves have a body temp of 109 in both human and shifted form. If they're out there now, I will know. Thank you for the warning." Professor Winters looks unconvinced.

"So what do we do now?" Loren asks. "Surely, we can't just go back to our room and ignore what we know is coming."

"That is exactly what you need to do. Nobody is getting in here. If an outside pack does gather outside our perimeters, it will only give us information on which pack we need to report to the council who governs us. For now, go to your rooms. Speak of this to no one. The last thing we need is any more students worrying."

"Randolph appreciates you bringing this matter to our attention. Now trust us to keep everyone safe," Professor Winter adds.

"Got it," I reply, spinning on my heel. We gave them the information, and that's all that we can do. Loren and Genesis follow me out.

"I don't know about you guys, but I'm not going to be able to rest tonight." Genesis finally says after several minutes into our walk back to the creek.

"I'm not going to bed," Loren agrees. "Thankfully, there are no classes tomorrow."

We finally make it back to the creek, and the entire gang is still where we left them. They've lit a fire in the center of the circle. We brief them on the conversation we had in Mr. Blakely's office—the one we weren't supposed to be sharing. Everyone states that they aren't comfortable with just going back to their dorm to sleep, so the plan is just to stay here.

"Does anyone want to address the big ass elephant in the room or, in this case, at the campfire?" Matt suggests.

"What, Matt?" Madison encourages.

"What happens if the pack actually gets through? What's our defense? We have to prepare for the worst and hope for the best."

"They'd have to face all of us. The whole school," one of the quiet girls says. "They can't take on vampires, witches, and the half gods. They'd be outnumbered in strength, numbers, and class, so none of this makes any sense."

"But that's just it. If what Elysian predicts is true, striking at first light makes the most sense. Who else knows about the impending attack besides us and the faculty? Most students will still be asleep. And if they have inside knowledge about when the cloak is scheduled to drop, then we can also assume they know that it would only be down for five minutes."

"Matt has a point," Madison agrees. "They will have a strategy— one to execute in less than five minutes. That's not enough time for the other students to recognize trouble in our midst and react. The attack will be over before they even realize what's going on."

"Although it may be accidental, being here by the creek is a strategy for us," Kristin informs. "If Genesis and Elysian are there primary targets, then they won't find them sleeping in their beds. The more time they take to look for them, the less time they have to execute their attack before the cloak goes back up. Either they'd abort or be stuck on this side to deal with being outnumbered."

"True, but what if half come for us and the other half seek out the pack here. Mitchell and Daniel both know where to find the alpha. The pack here are sitting ducks. I think we should warn them," I suggest.

I know Mr. Blakely told us not to alarm the other students, but I wouldn't feel right if things aren't intercepted, and the attack happens. It's partly my fault that they're coming. I'm the reason Jason ousted Mitchell and Daniel to the headmaster. I can't let them be blindsided.

"Maybe not the whole pack, but I'm in agreement with informing their alpha. Let him disseminate that info in the way he sees fit for them to be on guard. The only thing is ... our secret about how we get out will no longer be a secret."

"Not necessarily. Just because we share that the cloak drops at scheduled times doesn't automatically infer that we use that to leave campus. It's not that simple. Let's only share what we must. I know where he hangs out. I saw him playing pool in the campus lounge, and he's probably still there," Matt says. "I'll go check."

A swirl of wind whips around us, almost putting out the fire. I forgot that he was a vampire. He is only gone for a few minutes before he returns with Jason. I quickly fill him in on everything that's happened up to this point. He punches his fist inside his opposite hand several times, releasing a guttural growl each time.

"That little punk, Mitchell, has always wanted to be me. When he started sneaking his equally punk ass cousin onto campus, I should have known something was up. They're part of the Silvermane Pack. They're a medium-size pack but still a threat."

"Didn't want you guys to be sitting ducks should the attack happen," I admit.

"Dude, I appreciate that more than you know. I'll let my pack know that there's a possible attack coming our way as vengeance from Mitchell and Daniel. I'll share only what's necessary. We will begin our patrol of the perimeter a couple of hours before. They won't find us in bed, that's for sure," he growls again. "Whether it's me or you or both that they're coming for, we'll be ready in case they get through. We'll make them regret their decision to cross us."

He pats me on the back, nods at the rest of our circle, and disappears through the trees. Some of the weight has been lifted, knowing that the essential people involved know what's going on. Now I just hope that it doesn't come to an attack—that the faculty chooses not to let the cloak down.

CHAPTER TWENTY-TWO

Genesis

Soft snores sound across the nearly dim campfire. I shift my weight against Elysian who has been asleep for at least a couple of hours. I don't remember when I drifted off, but it was shortly after him. Elysian tenses underneath me— seconds before I hear it. An alarm shrills in the distance. *Loud and terrifying.* This was it— the moment we hoped wouldn't come. He hops to his feet, and we all follow his lead, our stance guarded. The sky is barely lit, but the impending danger is palpable. In a blink of an eye, we're surrounded. Ten wolves flank each other, forming a circle around us. Even on all fours, their height is nearly equal to ours standing. Their eyes glow with malice as their fangs drip with contempt. We're outnumbered by four. Kristin and Loren begin to chant in unison, but their incantation is no match for these wolves. They're both snatched and tossed aside like rag dolls. Their screams release one of my own. I want nothing more than to make sure they're okay, but we're stuck in this standoff. Each of their movements circle around us, keeping us on edge, waiting for them to ponce. I can sense Elysian's building anger, the twitch of his muscles before he makes his first move. Somehow, I just know that we're in sync, so I let my intuition into this fight.

Matt and Madison dash away from the scene with two of the wolves in pursuit, leaving Elysian and me to defend against the remaining eight. I don't get a chance to fear the impossible odds. Elysian does a backflip out of the circle and unleashes flames around their perimeter. I mimic his strategy by creating a ring of ice around me. The wolves are caught between fire and ice. It doesn't take long to see which element they'd rather avoid. The wolves swat through my ice fort with ease, their natural heat creating puddles of semi-melted ice around me. I'm knocked to my back, fangs mere inches from my face, when I hear a yelp from the one hovering over me.

"Genesis. Ice them," Elysian yells.

No further instruction is needed. He said *them* and not around them. He lights them on fire, and during their time of flailing, I'm free. I hop to my feet, and I begin to ice each of them—opposite of the location of the flames. Elysian ignites their bottom half as I block their top half in ice. My eyes bulge at the miraculous phenomenon unfolding in front of me. The wolves begin to shapeshift back into their human form where the ice has them frozen in place. My instinct is to continue my progression of glaciokinesis down toward their lower half. Elysian backs off his flames as my ice trail toward the feet. We have all eight wolves immobilized.

"We have to find the others," I suggest reluctantly, looking at the lifeless forms of Loren and Kristin.

There is no time to assess if they're okay. They're safe from further harm with the wolves we've blocked in their human forms. Now that Elysian and I have a system, we know what we must do to stop the others. Elysian dashes, and I'm on his heels. I can't think about how I'm doing any of this ... not now. The alarms continue to sound near the front of the campus, making it hard to decipher the location of the other attacks. Luckily, the rest of the pack is predictable. We find them already in combat with our campus pack. The trouble is, they're all in wolf form. How do we tell the bad guys from the good?

"Jason," Elysian calls out over the growls and yelps. "I need your pack to shapeshift back."

Nothing. The fighting continues in an evenly matched battle. That's about twenty wolves to distinguish between. Even with the increased numbers, we just brought the advantage. There are two of us free, and we just happen to know how to stop them in their tracks. Elysian targets one wolf out the pack, unleashing flames to the lower half. Following the needed sequence, I ice the top half until the fire and ice meets in a swirling blue and orange-reddish duo. As expected, the targeted wolf begins to transition into their human naked form. I continue the spread of the ice as Elysian backs off his flames. Before us in a block of ice, is Daniel. Elysian must have recognized his wolf form from his dream and personal attack.

A single howl signals a group of wolves to break apart from the fight and gather behind a single black wolf—their alpha. Elysian acts quickly, igniting the remaining ten wolves with fire as he dashes around them. I dash in the opposite direction, once again unleashing ice. The pack never stood a chance. Our element of surprise caught them off guard.

"Holy smokes," Madison says, appearing from nowhere. "Awesome thinking."

"Thanks for your help," I reply sarcastically.

"We were outnumbered, Genesis. Matt and I did what we thought was best."

"What? Run?"

"We ran to get some of the pack to follow us," Matt says, now appearing with Mr. Blakely and Professor Guenther. "We knew that we'd be faster, so we wanted as many of them to chase us to split them up ... to help even the odds."

"And we were able to lose them and get help," Madison adds.

"The wolves you left by the creek are being taken into custody now. The paddy wagon should be on the way to round up the rest of the pack here," Mr. Blakey informs.

"You all don't need to be here for the round up," Professor Guenther mentions. "Head to the gymnasium. The rest of the faculty will meet you there."

We retreat without further instruction. The pack

disappear ahead of us, I'm guessing to change back into their human form in private. Otherwise, there'd be hanging cocks everywhere and not just the ones currently blocked in ice. Elysian wraps an arm around my shoulder, and I startle.

"It's over," he assures. I stop mid-step as the events of the battle wash over me, the adrenaline gone. I begin to hyperventilate.

"Are you okay?" Madison asks, standing in front of me, trying to lift my chin.

"She's going to be fine. We'll catch up with you," he hints. "We're safe, babe. Just take nice deep breaths. It's over."

He lifts my chin and slides his lips over mine. He gives me a few soft pecks before I open for him. Gah, this man can kiss. I feel myself melt into him as he wraps his arms around me. Our lips finally separate as our foreheads meet.

"Thank you for that. It's just what I needed to get back to the here and now," I admit.

"I'll tell you a little secret." He smiles.

"What?"

"It may not be under the best circumstances, but I realized something out there."

"And what was that? Don't keep me in suspense."

"All I could think about is that I couldn't lose you. Then I realized I wasn't just falling in love with you, but that I already was. But that's not all. After I realized how I felt for you, I felt a surge of emotion. It caused another precognition, but this time I was awake for it. I knew what had to be done for us to win the battle. I knew that our powers would sync up to defeat them. I couldn't stop to explain it, but somehow, I knew that if you loved me too that it would work. My precognitions have yet to be wrong. But I still need to hear the words from your lips."

"What words?" I tease. I knew what he meant. He gives me a fake pout and makes tonight's attack begin to fade. This beautiful, powerful man just admitted that he was in love with me. "Well, since we're being all truthful, I can admit that I've felt something. I didn't want to admit I was falling because we never put a label on what we were doing. I didn't want to set myself up for heartbreak."

"And now?"

"And now, I think my heart knew all along what my brain was trying to protect me from. I'm irrevocably in love with you, Mr. Remis."

"I think both of our hearts knew before we could admit it to ourselves. We're entangled ... that should have been our first clue. We found our way to each other. Love was always destined for us. We just had to let it in."

"I love your hypothesis, babe. But we need to get to the gym now that my mild freak-out is over."

"Mild, eh?" he teases. I shove him playfully. "You just needed my lips. I have other parts at your service if needed."

"Come on, weirdo."

I link my arms through his as we head to the gym.

The assembly is brief and to the point. The faculty

does a thorough head count of the students to ensure that we're all safe and accounted for. Mr. Blakely announces that changes are coming for the academy as a whole due to tonight's attack. All classes are canceled tomorrow, and another assembly is scheduled for two. Incessant chatter fills the gym as we try to guess what these changes are and how they will affect us. We are dismissed after we're assured that we are safe. There is no mention of what is in store for the wolves they've rounded up. No mention if they let the veil down or how the wolves were able to breach the campus even with the warning Elysian gave them. I don't feel safe. Sensing, my doubt, Elysian pulls me closer to him.

"I'm not leaving you alone. I'm coming to your room, and I don't care who sees."

"But the curfew—"

"I don't give a fuck about a curfew. They owe us more of an explanation than the one we just got. I know it's late ... well, technically early since the sun is rising, but I hope they have more answers for us later today after the dust settles. Until then, I'm not leaving your side."

I don't bother arguing with him. I feel safer with him—not by the faculty's empty promises. We stop by the infirmary to check on Loren and Kristin before heading back to my room. Professor Winters is there with a few other women who I haven't met. Candles flickers around the two stretchers that they're on. Herbs and artifacts are spread on the floor between them. It doesn't take a genius to figure out that these women aren't practicing modern medicine here. They're witches.

"You two can't be here," Professor Winters informs as she walks up to us. "I know you're worried, but the girls are going to be just fine."

"But—"

"No buts, dear. Go back to your rooms."

She doesn't leave us much choice. She ushers us out and closes the door behind her. An audible click of the lock discourages us from trying to reenter. For now, we'll have to take her word that the girls will be okay. I hope whatever witchcraft they're performing works. I feel so helpless, but I'm thankful to have Elysian by my side. We'll see how this all works out tomorrow.

EPILOGUE

Elysian

Genesis and I barely slept. She was worried about Kristin and Loren, and I was too. It killed me that I couldn't completely ease her mind. She looked somewhat hopeful when she received a text from Loren an hour ago to save her a seat at this assembly. We haven't talked with the rest of the Elite since this all went down, but I'm sure we'll come together after we hear what these changes are going to be. We take our seat near the front of the podium. We're both surprised when Loren slides into the seat next to us about ten minutes later. Both of the girls hug and wipe away their tears as I look on. I want to ask how she is feeling, but we're interrupted by a tap on the mic. But that's not what gets my attention. Loren spots them too.

"Who is that?" she asks.

"Where?" Genesis asks.

I point at the two students that have just taken a front

row seat next to Professor Guenther. I don't know every student here, but they look new. Loren doesn't recognize them either, and she knows everybody.

"Why are they dressed like us?" Genesis inquires after finally spotting them.

And there it is. The *conundrum*. Not because they're two new students, but because they're dressed like us. They've been outfitted in the very uniform that has been reserved for our class. We're the only two half gods here, so why are they wearing our uniform?

"And there are two of them," I point out.

"Do you think they're half gods too— entangled like us. Are they a pair?"

She has hit all my unasked questions on the nose. They have to be the same class as us ... right? But if the other stuff is true, then what does this mean? Are there more of us on Earth than the faculty originally thought? Are we related?

"Let me have your attention," Mr. Blakely begins, but it's hard to focus. So many mind fucks in so little time.

"I'm going to start by explaining what happened with the breach this morning and then what our plan is moving forward."

Genesis reaches over and pulls my hand into hers, forcing me to tamper down my racing thoughts long enough to listen. Mr. Blakely explains that they had an anonymous tip that the wolves were coming and that an attack was imminent, but he doesn't share that the tip was from me. He further explains that the wolves were strategic. They knew that they had to blend in with the employees already waiting for the veil to come down for work. They wore cooling vest to lower their body temperatures to normal range. They also knew that if a scan was used, it would detect a body count. With the tip the faculty had, they scanned the woods via drone for heat signals and the appropriate body count. The veil left them blind to the wolves that were hiding amongst the workers because they snatched twenty of the workers prior to their arrival and took their place to get in. The veil in this instance was a hinderance, so therefore it's coming down. *Permanently*. There is a collective gasp heard around the auditorium.

Security measures will be more thorough, but they're going to relax the rules of students leaving and returning to campus. They believe the loopholes students may have found to sneak off campus is also how the perpetrators found a loophole onto the campus.

"Shit," Loren curses. "I hope this wasn't our fault."

"So what does this mean?" Genesis asks.

"It means he's looking to run our campus like Legends Academy. They've always been an open campus. Humans even know that the school exist. The students come and go as they please, with curfew of course, but nothing like here."

Mr. Blakely confirms that is his intent. He wants to make our campus comparable to Legends. The faculty of the two schools are meeting this week to discuss aligning our practices and identifying ways to keep the students safe with an open campus.

"This is huge," Loren confirms. "Legends is accredited because the humans know that the academy exists. That means that if our campus takes the accreditation route, you can transfer your classes here. This is good news for us all. We can actually graduate from this school."

"That would be amazing, but personally, I want to graduate from the school I put all my effort into," I say.

"Me too," Genesis agrees. "No offense."

"None taken." Loren shrugs. "It's just an option and a dream come true for many of us. But it's more than just the degree. Imagine not having to wait to earn privileges to leave campus or have friends visit. Your family could visit. It would be like a normal college experience instead of being some hidden away secret. It's about time that they treated us like the Legends' students. I just hate that this had to happen for my uncle to give it any real thought."

"Well, let's not get ahead of ourselves or our hopes up. Let's wait to see how much of the other academy practices they adopt. It would be great to have my family and friends visit, but how soon will they make the change?"

"Elysian is right. They may meet with the other school and decide not to do things exactly the same. But at least it's a possibility." She looks over at Loren. "Are you okay? I know you're sitting here, but I saw what happened last night. I thought you and Kristin were going to die."

"We're both fine. It's one of the perks of being taken

care of by some powerful witches. Sort of like your self-healing thing, but with portions and spells."

"I'm just glad that the two of you are okay," Genesis admits. "Now we need to get to the bottom of who these new students are."

Mr. Blakely continues to talk, but our focus has shifted to the blonde girl and raven-haired guy. Their backs are to us, but they didn't look stoic to be here. The faculty doesn't bother introducing them either. If it weren't for the uniforms, I wouldn't have taken them for students here.

Suddenly the blonde turns in her seat. Her eyes lock with mine in an uncomfortable stare off. So much so the guy turns to follow her gaze. I nudge Genesis and now we're in a four-way stare. Mr. Blakely dismisses us so I quickly stand.

"Let's get out of here," I tell the girls. "If those two are one of us, we'll know soon enough."

"If they are like us, I wonder what their power is? Would they be able to manipulate fire and ice like us? What if you decide you like her better than me?" she rambles. "Even from a distance, I can see she is gorgeous."

"Not a chance, babe. You're my girlfriend, and you're stuck with me," I assure.

"When did this girlfriend thing happen? I don't remember you asking," she teases.

"Probably when he stuck his meat stick inside your—"

"Loren!" Genesis squeals, embarrassed.

"Well, she isn't lying." I chuckle.

"You two are insufferable."

"But you love me." A lump forms in my throat. Admitting my emotions is something that I'll have to get more comfortable with. I'm allowing myself to be vulnerable with her. Yes, we've talked about love as a result of our entanglement, but this all feels so surreal. This is what love feels like and I'm all in.

She stops mid-stride. "I do. I do love you, Elysian."

Her nearly clear eyes pierce mine, and I feel my heart slam against my chest. This beautiful girl just admitted that she loves me. I square my shoulders and pull her to me once again. Everything and everyone fade into the background.

"I love you, Genesis Aldaine. Will you be my girlfriend?"

"Yes. I can't think of a better person I'd rather be stuck with. I'm yours."

I tip her chin back and lick the seam of her lips. She opens for me, and I passionately swirl her tongue with mine. I forget that we're standing in the middle of the campus until Loren clears her throat. I'm about to give her shit for the interruption since she's the one who's been pushing us together from the start, but then I see them. The duo from the assembly. The girl stares off into the distance, avoiding eye contact. The guy sizes me up but doesn't speak. They're both with Mr. Blakely.

"Genesis and Elysian, I need you to come with us," he informs, ominously.

"What's this about? "Genesis asks. "Are they the same as us?"

"We're standing right here," the guy deadpans. "And we have names."

"Genesis. Elysian. This is Imogen and Rhys." Neither of us shakes hands or exchanges pleasantries. The two don't give off the friendliest of vibes.

"Watch how you speak to my girl, *Rhys*," I address.

"Cut the pissing contest," Mr. Blakely warns. "We need to get to my office. Now. There is much to discuss."

His nostrils flare, and I know that he means business. I fall in step with him and the two newbies with attitudes. I give Genesis's hand a soft squeeze. I don't know who these two are, or if they're, in fact, half gods, but it doesn't matter. I have the girl who just professed her love to me minutes ago. Anything else Mr. Blakely is waiting to throw at us is small potatoes. What's the worst that he can tell us?

Thank you for reading Quantum Entanglement: Part One. Are you ready to meet Imogen and Rhys? What does their arrival at the Legion of Supernatural Academy mean? What changes are coming and are the students still in danger? Find out in Quantum Entanglement: Part Two. Preorder now to take advantage of our special pre-release price. You don't want to miss the epic continuation of twisted tales and suspense - driven fantasy.

Preorder Quantum Entanglement: Part 2 now —> http://bit.ly/QE2aeb

Join our Watson & Stacks' Newsletter to be the first to learn about our upcoming releases, giveaways, and more:

Our VIP-> http://bit.ly/2ELBM73

QUANTUM ENTANGLEMENT: PART ONE PLAYLIST

Grow – LAQUD
  Better than Today – Rhys Lewis
  Enjoy the Silence - Anberlin
  Sleep Alone – Bat for Lashes
  Head Over Heels – Digital Daggers
  Tilikum – Benjamin Francis Leftwich
  Run – Leona Lewis
  Lovely (with Khalid) – Billie Eilish
  Bloodstream – Stateless
  Broken Strings – James Morrison & Nelly Furtado
  Human – Civil Twilight
  Twice - Little Dragon
  King Youngblood – Gypsy Temple
  Smother – Daughter
  Happening – Olivia Broadfield
  Eyes on Fire – Blue Foundation
  Fickle Game – Amber Run

Pictures of You – Elizabeth Harper

Eyes Without a Face – Billy Idol

Everything Little Thing She Does is Magic – Sleeping at Last

Human – Rag 'n 'Bone Man

Do You Remember – Jarryd James & Raury

Truth is a beautiful Thing - London Grammar

Not Real Anymore – Dreaming of Ghosts, Robot Koch & Fiora

Loveeeeeee Song – Rihanna

Come Undone – Duran Duran

OTHER BOOKS BY S.R. WATSON & RYAN STACKS

S.I.N. Rock Star Trilogy

Sex in Numbers - Book #1

Creed of Redemption - Book #2

Leave it All Behind - Book #3

The Playboy's Lair Duet

Silas: A Playboy's Lair Novel – Part One

Silas: A Playboy's Lair Novel – Part Two

Forbidden Trilogy

Forbidden Attraction - Book #1

Forbidden Love - Book #2

Unforbidden - Book #3

Stand Alone

The Object of His Desire

Mister English

Peppermint Mocha Love: A Christmas Novella (written as S. Renee' ... co-authored with R.L. Harmon)

Her Favorite Christmas Gift (written as S. Renee' ... co-authored with R.L. Harmon)

ABOUT S.R. WATSON

USA Today Bestselling Author, S. R. Watson, is a Texas native who currently resides in Washington with her children. She grew up reading the Sweet Valley series (Twins, High, & University) among others. Although she wrote countless stories during high school, she'd never published any of them. She continued her education and became an operating room registered nurse. The pursuit towards earning her degrees, meant less time for leisure reading and writing for a bit. After picking up reading again, starting with the Twilight series and 50 Shades Trilogy, she decided to pursue her passion for writing once again.

S. R. Watson (also writes as S. Reneé) published her first book in 2014. She is the author of the Forbidden Trilogy, The Object of His Desire, and the co-authored S.I.N. Trilogy. She co-authored Peppermint Mocha Love, R.L. Harmon (also writes as Ryan Stacks). The duo also collaborated on Unforbidden and Silas Part Two with more to come.

When S. R. Watson is not writing, or working as travel

OR nurse, she loves to read and binge watch her favorite shows (Scandal, Elementary, Big Brother, etc.)

ABOUT RYAN STACKS

USA Today Bestselling Author, Ryan Stacks, is a Washington native who currently resides in Kennewick with his wife Anna Harmon. Most would consider him a jack of all trades. His first love is wrestling and he's wrestled his entire life. In addition to his talents on the mat, Ryan has many achievements. He's a published international cover model and he released his first book, Peppermint Mocha Love with co-author, S. Reneé in December 2017. For this novella, he debuted as both an author and cover photographer. Ryan Stacks has partnered with S.R. Watson (also writes as as S. Reneé) to create more stories under his current pen name as well as R.L. Harmon.

When Ryan Stacks is not writing, he spends his time helping to build the wrestling sport within the community as one of the coaches for Richland High School as well as a youth program. In addition to his commitment to the community, Ryan has taken his fitness career to new highs as a men's physique competitor - placing top 3 at the national level.

Made in the USA
Las Vegas, NV
17 August 2021